JOHN OSBORNE

Look Back in Anger

ff

FABER & FABER

First published in 1957
by Faber & Faber Limited
74–77 Great Russell Street
London WC1B 3DA
First published in this edition 1960; reset 1996
This paperback edition first published in 2015

Photoset by Parker Typesetting Service, Leicester
Printed and bound by CPI Group (UK) Ltd, Croydon, CRO 4YY

A CIP record for this book is available from the British Library

ISBN 978-0-571-32276-3

For
MY FATHER

Contents

Introduction

In the summer of 1955 an advertisement appeared in *The Stage* newspaper asking for new plays. It had been placed by the English Stage Company, which was setting up in business at an unfashionable theatre, the Royal Court, in London's Sloane Square. The response to the ad was tremendous. Seven hundred and fifty scripts poured in. The only trouble was, most of them were rubbish: either bottom-drawer pieces by hack writers or, in the words of Tony Richardson, who was to become the ESC's Associate Director, 'endless blank-verse shit'.

Only one piece leapt out of the pile: the curiously entitled *Look Back in Anger* by a totally unknown young actor called John Osborne. George Devine, the founding father of the ESC and its first director, read the play in the study of his riverside house in Hammersmith and immediately sniffed its promise. He took it to Richardson, who lodged in the flat upstairs, who was even more smitten by it. Together they made a commitment to produce it in their first season at the Royal Court in 1956.

But who exactly was John Osborne? To find out, Devine made the unusual decision to track the author to his lair. He discovered the writer was living in a leaky old Rhine barge, moored near Chiswick Bridge, which he shared with a fellow-actor, Anthony Creighton. So on a hot afternoon in August 1955, because the tide was high, Devine was obliged to borrow a boat and row himself out to the Osborne residence. He quizzed him eagerly and discovered that Osborne was a hard-up twenty-six-year-old actor who had slogged his way round the regional reps, had written part of *Look Back in Anger* while sitting in a deckchair on Morecambe Pier and was separated from his actress-wife, Pamela Lane. By the end of the afternoon, Devine had offered Osborne £25 for a year's option on his play. What neither man could have realised was that they were helping to make theatrical history.

But Osborne had to bide his time. The ESC didn't officially take over the Royal Court until April 1956. Its mission was quite clear: to provide a counterweight to the quilted divertissements of the West End by unearthing new British plays and exposing audiences to the best work from abroad. Having recently visited Brecht's Berliner Ensemble, Devine also wanted to change the whole style of British theatre. Lavish pictorial scenery was to be banished. Its place was to be taken by design that, on the Brechtian model, was to be spare, rigorous and beautiful. There was even a covert sexual agenda and an attempt to rid British theatre of its pervasive air of camp: something that was achieved with a team of associate directors who were all, as it happens, privately gay.

There was, however, no overnight Royal Court revolution. The opening production, in April 1956, was of Angus Wilson's *The Mulberry Bush*: a decent, middle-class play by an admired novelist that failed to generate much excitement. The second choice, Arthur Miller's *The Crucible*, was more successful but revealed little about the Royal Court's policy. Then, on 8 May 1956, *Look Back in Anger* had its premiere. It is a date that has now entered the history books but, according to Osborne's own testimony in his memoir, *Almost A Gentleman*, there was little sense at the time that anything momentous had occurred. Only later would that date acquire the status of legend. In fact, the reviews in the daily papers were not as disastrous as theatrical myth suggests. *The Times*, the *Daily Telegraph* and the London evening papers were all decidedly negative. But Philip Hope-Wallace in the *Manchester Guardian* was cautiously approving ('I believe they have got a potential playwright at last'), John Barber in the *Daily Express* got highly excited (describing the play as 'intense, angry, feverish, undisciplined' but also 'young, young, young') and Derek Granger in the *Financial Times* was intelligently appreciative ('its influence should go far beyond such an eccentric and isolated one-man turn as *Waiting for Godot*'). The trouble was that the *FT* didn't sell many tickets. I have a touch of sympathy with the overnight critics: I know how difficult it is to absorb, describe and evaluate a game-changing new play against a merciless deadline. But on the following Sunday the whole tone changed. Kenneth Tynan wrote a much-quoted review in the *Observer* that unequivocally turned Osborne into a spokesman for the disaffected young and that ringingly declared: 'I doubt if I could love anyone who did not wish to see *Look Back in Anger*.' Harold Hobson in the *Sunday Times* was more restrained, but dubbed Osborne 'a writer of outstanding promise'.

Even with the imprimatur of Tynan and Hobson, the play was not an instant hit. But two events gave the play a fresh momentum. One was the fact that BBC Television showed an eighteen-minute extract which led to the box-office being besieged. The other was the decision by a young Faber editor, Charles Monteith, to ask Osborne's permission to publish the play at a time when few stage scripts achieved that kind of permanence. In fact, only a month after the opening night Monteith wrote to Osborne saying, 'I haven't enjoyed an evening in the theatre so much for a very long time indeed,' and going on to ask if he might be interested in writing a novel. No fiction ever transpired. But this was the start of a long and lasting relationship in which Faber went on to publish the entire Osborne canon. It was also a significant moment in that it established the idea that play-texts should become a vital part of the publishing agenda. I can vouch for the importance of that since I still have my own dog-eared copy of the original paperback edition of *Look Back in Anger*. I can also testify to the play's impact. I was a sixteen-year-old Midlands schoolboy when the play first appeared but I became obsessed both by the work itself and the whole Angry Young Man phenomenon it supposedly represented. I have written before of how, coming to see the play at one of its many revivals in 1957, I stood outside the Royal Court gazing at the faces of people emerging from the Saturday first-house performance to see if they had been visibly changed by the event.

But why did *Look Back in Anger* make the impact it did? The first, and most obvious point, is that it put so much of 1950s England on stage. Through the eloquent arias – 'not "tirades"' insists Osborne – of Jimmy Porter, it tackles sex, class, religion, politics, the press and the sense of a country stifled by an official, establishment culture. What few of us realised at the time was that Osborne, while endorsing most of Jimmy's jeremiads, also had a sneaking sympathy for his father-in-law, Colonel Redfern, an upper-class relic of the Raj. Alison, Jimmy's wife, tells her father: 'You're hurt because everything is changed. Jimmy is hurt because everything is the same.' I think she's half right in that, while the colonialist Colonel grieves over an

Edwardian paradise lost, Jimmy is an angry romantic nostalgic for a world he never knew. In the 1950s the play was prized, above all, as a social document: an eloquent testament of alienated youth. Later it came to be seen as a Strindbergian study of a marriage steeped in love and hate. But, increasingly, I suspect Osborne's real revolution lay in liberating theatrical language. Osborne himself has written of his despair, as a young actor, of trying to learn Somerset Maugham's dialogue: 'Dead, elusively inert, wobbly like some synthetic rubber substance,' was his typically damning phrase. But Osborne's language is thrillingly alive and calls on a variety of sources ranging from Bunyanesqe moral rigour (note the emphasis on words like 'fire' and 'blood') to the rat-a-tat repetitions of the music-hall and the sexual candour of D. H. Lawrence. Osborne showed that theatrical prose could achieve its own distinctive poetry and among the beneficiaries were writers as diverse as Harold Pinter, John Arden and Peter Gill. More immediately, the success of *Look Back in Anger* gave the Royal Court a pivotal status in British culture and encouraged successive generations to turn to playwriting. Some, such as Arnold Wesker and Ann Jellicoe, were Osborne's contemporaries. Others, such as David Hare, Christopher Hampton and Howard Brenton, were products of later decades who burned with a theatrical ambition that Osborne himself had kindled. It is easy to sneer at the journalistic concept of the Angry Young Man (a phrase, incidentally, coined by a dismissive Royal Court press officer). But what is unarguable is that *Look Back in Anger*, through its blazing immediacy, corrosive vitality and linguistic exuberance, changed British theatre. In the words of Alan Sillitoe, 'John Osborne didn't contribute to British theatre: he set off a landmine called *Look Back in Anger* and blew most of it up. The bits have settled back into place, of course, but it can never be the same again.'

MICHAEL BILLINGTON,
2014

Cast in order of appearance

Jimmy Porter
Cliff Lewis
Alison Porter
Helena Charles
Colonel Redfern

The action throughout takes place in the
Porters' one-room flat in the Midlands.

TIME: The present.

ACT I
Early Evening. April

ACT II
Scene 1: Two weeks later.
Scene 2: The following evening.

ACT III
Scene 1: Several months later.
Scene 2: A few minutes later.

Look Back in Anger was first performed at the Royal Court Theatre, Sloane Square, London, on 8 May 1956, by the English Stage Company. The cast was as follows:

Jimmy Porter Kenneth Haigh
Cliff Lewis Alan Bates
Alison Porter Mary Ure
Helena Charles Helena Hughes
Colonel Redfern John Welsh

Directed by Tony Richardson
Décor by Alan Tagg

LOOK BACK IN ANGER

Act I

The Porters' one-room flat in a large Midland town. Early evening. April.

The scene is a fairly large attic room, at the top of a large Victorian house. The ceiling slopes down quite sharply from L to R. Down R are two small low windows. In front of these is a dark oak dressing table. Most of the furniture is simple, and rather old. Up R is a double bed, running the length of most of the back wall, the rest of which is taken up with a shelf of books. Down R below the bed is a heavy chest of drawers, covered with books, neckties and odds and ends, including a large, tattered toy teddy bear and soft, woolly squirrel. Up L is a door. Below this a small wardrobe. Most of the wall L is taken up with a high, oblong window. This looks out on to the landing, but light comes through it from a skylight beyond. Below the wardrobe is a gas stove, and, beside this, a wooden food cupboard, on which is a small, portable radio. Down C is a sturdy dining table and three chairs, and, below this, L and R, two deep, shabby leather armchairs.

At rise of curtain, **Jimmy** *and* **Cliff** *are seated in the two armchairs R and L, respectively. All that we can see of either of them is two pairs of legs, sprawled way out beyond the newspapers which hide the rest of them from sight. They are both reading. Beside them, and between them, is a jungle of newspapers and weeklies. When we do eventually see them, we find that Jimmy is a tall, thin young man about twenty-five, wearing a very worn tweed jacket and flannels. Clouds of smoke fill the room from the pipe he is smoking. He is a disconcerting mixture of sincerity and cheerful malice, of tenderness and freebooting cruelty; restless, importunate, full of pride, a combination which alienates the sensitive and insensitive alike. Blistering honesty, or apparent honesty, like*

*his, makes few friends. To many he may seem sensitive to the
point of vulgarity. To others, he is simply a loudmouth. To
be as vehement as he is is to be almost non-committal. Cliff is
the same age, short, dark, big boned, wearing a pullover and
grey, new, but very creased trousers. He is easy and relaxed,
almost to lethargy, with the rather sad, natural intelligence of
the self-taught. If Jimmy alienates love, Cliff seems to exact it
– demonstrations of it, at least, even from the cautious. He is
a soothing, natural counterpoint to Jimmy.*

Standing L, below the food cupboard, is **Alison.** *She is
leaning over an ironing board. Beside her is a pile of clothes.
Hers is the most elusive personality to catch in the uneasy
polyphony of these three people. She is turned in a different
key, a key of well-bred malaise that is often drowned in the
robust orchestration of the other two. Hanging over the
grubby, but expensive, skirt she is wearing is a cherry red
shirt of Jimmy's, but she manages somehow to look quite
elegant in it. She is roughly the same age as the men.
Somehow, their combined physical oddity makes her beauty
more striking than it really is. She is tall, slim, dark. The
bones of her face are long and delicate. There is a surprising
reservation about her eyes, which are so large and deep they
should make equivocation impossible. The room is still,
smoke-filled. The only sound is the occasional thud of
Alison's iron on the board. It is one of those chilly spring
evenings, all cloud and shadows. Presently, Jimmy throws his
paper down.*

Jimmy Why do I do this every Sunday? Even the book
reviews seem to be the same as last week's. Different books –
same reviews. Have you finished that one yet?

Cliff Not yet.

Jimmy I've just read three whole columns on the English
Novel. Half of it's in French. Do the Sunday papers make *you*
feel ignorant?

2

Cliff Not 'arf.

Jimmy Well, you *are* ignorant. You're just a peasant. (*to Alison*) What about you? You're not a peasant are you?

Alison (*absently*) What's that?

Jimmy I said do the papers make you feel you're not so brilliant after all?

Alison Oh – I haven't read them yet.

Jimmy I didn't ask you that. I said –

Cliff Leave the poor girlie alone. She's busy.

Jimmy Well, she can talk, can't she? You can talk, can't you? You can express an opinion. Or does the White Woman's Burden make it impossible to think?

Alison I'm sorry. I wasn't listening properly.

Jimmy You bet you weren't listening. Old Porter talks, and everyone turns over and goes to sleep. And Mrs Porter gets 'em all going with the first yawn.

Cliff Leave her alone, I said.

Jimmy (*shouting*) All right, dear. Go back to sleep. It was only me talking. You know? Talking? Remember? I'm sorry.

Cliff Stop yelling. I'm trying to read.

Jimmy Why do you bother? You can't understand a word of it.

Cliff Uh huh.

Jimmy You're too ignorant.

Cliff Yes, and uneducated. Now shut up, will you?

Jimmy Why don't you get my wife to explain it to you? She's educated. (*to her*) That's right, isn't it?

Cliff (*kicking out at him from behind his paper*) Leave her alone, I said.

Jimmy Do that again, you Welsh ruffian, and I'll pull your ears off.

He bangs Cliff's paper out of his hands.

Cliff (*leaning forward*) Listen – I'm trying to better myself. Let me get on with it, you big, horrible man. Give it me. (*Puts his hand out for paper.*)

Alison Oh, give it to him, Jimmy, for heaven's sake! I can't think!

Cliff Yes, come on, give me the paper. She can't think.

Jimmy Can't think! (*Throws the paper back at him.*) She hasn't had a thought for years! Have you?

Alison No.

Jimmy (*picks up a weekly*) I'm getting hungry.

Alison Oh no, not already!

Cliff He's a bloody pig.

Jimmy I'm not a pig. I just like food – that's all.

Cliff Like it! You're like a sexual maniac – only with you it's food. You'll end up in the *News of the World*, boyo, you wait. James Porter, aged twenty-five, was bound over last week after pleading guilty to interfering with a small cabbage and two tins of beans on his way home from the Builder's Arms. The accused said he hadn't been feeling well for some time, and had been having black-outs. He asked for his good record as an air-raid warden, second class, to be taken into account.

Jimmy (*grins*) Oh, yes, yes, yes. I like to eat. I'd like to live too. Do you mind?

Cliff Don't see any use in your eating at all. You never get any fatter.

Jimmy People like me don't get fat. I've tried to tell you before. We just burn everything up. Now shut up while I read. You can make me some more tea.

Cliff Good God, you've just had a great potful! I only had one cup.

Jimmy Like hell! Make some more.

Cliff (*to Alison*) Isn't that right? Didn't I only have one cup?

Alison (*without looking up*) That's right.

Cliff There you are. And she only had one cup too. I saw her. You guzzled the lot.

Jimmy (*reading his weekly*) Put the kettle on.

Cliff Put it on yourself. You've creased up my paper.

Jimmy I'm the only one who knows how to treat a paper, or anything else, in this house. (*Picks up another paper.*) Girl here wants to know whether her boy friend will lose all respect for her if she gives him what he asks for. Stupid bitch.

Cliff Just let me get at her, that's all.

Jimmy Who buys this damned thing? (*throws it down*) Haven't you read the other posh paper yet?

Cliff Which?

Jimmy Well, there are only two posh papers on a Sunday – the one you're reading, and this one. Come on, let me have that one, and you take this.

Cliff Oh, all right.

They exchange.

I was only reading the Bishop of Bromley. (*puts out his hand to Alison*) How are you, dullin'?

Alison All right thank you, dear.

Cliff (*grasping her hand*) Why don't you leave all that, and sit down for a bit? You look tired.

Alison (*smiling*) I haven't much more to do.

Cliff (*kisses her hand, and puts her fingers in his mouth*) She's a beautiful girl, isn't she?

Jimmy That's what they all tell me.

His eyes meet hers.

Cliff It's a lovely, delicious paw you've got. Ummmmm. I'm going to bite it off.

Alison Don't! I'll burn his shirt.

Jimmy Give her her finger back, and don't be so sickening. What's the Bishop of Bromley say?

Cliff (*letting go of Alison*) Oh, it says here that he makes a very moving appeal to all Christians to do all they can to assist in the manufacture of the H-Bomb.

Jimmy Yes, well, that's quite moving, I suppose. (*to Alison*) Are you moved, my darling?

Alison Well, naturally.

Jimmy There you are: even my wife is moved. I ought to send the Bishop a subscription. Let's see. What else does he say. Dumdidumdidumdidum. Ah yes. He's upset because someone has suggested that he supports the rich against the poor. He says he denies the difference of class distinction. 'This idea has been persistently and wickedly fostered by – the working classes!' Well!

He looks up at both of them for reaction, but Cliff is

6

reading, and Alison is intent on her ironing.

(*to Cliff*) Did you read that bit?

Cliff Um?

He has lost them, and he knows it, but he won't leave it.

Jimmy (*to Alison*) You don't suppose your father could have written it, do you?

Alison Written what?

Jimmy What I just read out, of course.

Alison Why should my father have written it?

Jimmy Sounds rather like Daddy, don't you think?

Alison Does it?

Jimmy Is the Bishop of Bromley his nom de plume, do you think?

Cliff Don't take any notice of him. He's being offensive. And it's so easy for him.

Jimmy (*quickly*) Did you read about the woman who went to the mass meeting of a certain American evangelist at Earls Court? She went forward, to declare herself for love or whatever it is, and, in the rush of converts to get to the front, she broke four ribs and got kicked in the head. She was yelling her head off in agony, but with 50,000 people putting all they'd got into 'Onward Christian Soldiers', nobody even knew she was there.

He looks up sharply for a response, but there isn't any.

Sometimes, I wonder if there isn't something wrong with me. What about that tea?

Cliff (*still behind paper*) What tea?

Jimmy Put the kettle on.

Alison looks up at him.

Alison Do you want some more tea?

Jimmy I don't know. No, I don't think so.

Alison Do you want some, Cliff?

Jimmy No, he doesn't. How much longer will you be doing that?

Alison Won't be long.

Jimmy God, how I hate Sundays! It's always so depressing, always the same. We never seem to get any further, do we? Always the same ritual. Reading the papers, drinking tea, ironing. A few more hours, and another week gone. Our youth is slipping away. Do you know that?

Cliff (*throws down paper*) What's that?

Jimmy (*casually*) Oh, nothing, nothing. Damn you, damn both of you, damn them all.

Cliff Let's go to the pictures. (*to Alison*) What do you say, lovely?

Alison I don't think I'll be able to. Perhaps Jimmy would like to go. (*to Jimmy*) Would you like to?

Jimmy And have my enjoyment ruined by the Sunday night yobs in the front row? No, thank you. (*pause*) Did you read Priestley's piece this week? Why on earth I ask I don't know. I know damned well you haven't. Why do I spend ninepence on that damned paper every week? Nobody reads it except me. Nobody can be bothered. No one can raise themselves out of their delicious sloth. You two will drive me round the bend soon – I know it, as sure as I'm sitting here. I know you're going to drive me mad. Oh heavens, how I long for a little ordinary human enthusiasm. Just enthusiasm – that's all. I want to hear a warm, thrilling voice cry out Hallelujah! (*He* *bangs his breast theatrically.*) Hallelujah! I'm alive! I've an idea. Why don't we have a little game? Let's pretend that we're human beings, and that we're actually alive. Just for a while. What do you say? Let's pretend we're human. (*He looks from one to the other.*) Oh, brother, it's such a long time since I was with anyone who got enthusiastic about anything.

Cliff What did he say?

Jimmy (*resentful of being dragged away from his pursuit of Alison*) What did who say?

Cliff Mr Priestley.

Jimmy What he always says, I suppose. He's like Daddy – still casting well-fed glances back to the Edwardian twilight from his comfortable, disenfranchized wilderness. What the devil have you done to those trousers?

Cliff Done?

Jimmy Are they the ones you bought last week-end? Look at them. Do you see what he's done to those new trousers?

Alison You are naughty, Cliff. They look dreadful.

Jimmy You spend good money on a new pair of trousers, and then sprawl about in them like a savage. What do you think you're going to do when I'm not around to look after you? Well, what are you going to do? Tell me?

Cliff (*grinning*) I don't know. (*to Alison*) What am I going to do, lovely?

Alison You'd better take them off.

Jimmy Yes, go on. Take 'em off. And I'll kick your behind for you.

Alison I'll give them a press while I've got the iron on.

Cliff OK (*starts taking them off*) I'll just empty the pockets. (*takes out keys, matches, handkerchief*)

Jimmy Give me those matches, will you?

Cliff Oh, you're not going to start up that old pipe again, are you? It stinks the place out. (*to Alison*) Doesn't it smell awful?

Jimmy grabs the matches, and lights up.

Alison I don't mind it. I've got used to it.

Jimmy She's a great one for getting used to things. If she were to die, and wake up in paradise – after the first five minutes, she'd have got used to it.

Cliff (*hands her the trousers*) Thank you, lovely. Give me a cigarette, will you?

Jimmy Don't give him one.

Cliff I can't stand the stink of that old pipe any longer. I must have a cigarette.

Jimmy I thought the doctor said no cigarettes?

Cliff Oh, why doesn't he shut up?

Jimmy All right. They're your ulcers. Go ahead, and have a bellyache, if that's what you want. I give up. I give up. I'm sick of doing things for people. And all for what?

Alison gives Cliff a cigarette. They both light up, and she goes on with her ironing.

Nobody thinks, nobody cares. No beliefs, no convictions and no enthusiasm. Just another Sunday evening.

Cliff sits down again, in his pullover and shorts.

Perhaps there's a concert on. (*Picks up* Radio Times.) Ah. (*nudges Cliff with his foot*) Make some more tea.

Cliff grunts. He is reading again.

Oh, yes. There's a Vaughan Williams. Well, that's something, anyway. Something strong, something simple, something English. I suppose people like me aren't supposed to be very patriotic. Somebody said – what was it – we get our cooking from Paris (that's a laugh), our politics from Moscow, and our morals from Port Said. Something like that, anyway. Who was it? (*pause*) Well, you wouldn't know anyway. I hate to admit it, but I think I can understand how her Daddy must have felt when he came back from India, after all those years away. The old Edwardian brigade do make their brief little world look pretty tempting. All home-make cakes and croquet, bright ideas, bright uniforms. Always the same picture: high summer, the long days in the sun, slim volumes of verse, crisp linen, the smell of starch. What a romantic picture. Phoney too, of course. It must have rained sometimes. Still, even I regret it somehow, phoney or not. If you've no world of your own, it's rather pleasant to regret the passing of someone else's. I must be getting sentimental. But I must say it's pretty dreary living in the American Age – unless you're an American of course. Perhaps all our children will be Americans. That's a thought isn't it?

He gives Cliff a kick, and shouts at him.

I said that's a thought!

Cliff You did?

Jimmy You sit there like a lump of dough. I thought you were going to make me some tea.

Cliff groans. Jimmy turns to Alison.

Is your friend Webster coming tonight?

Alison He might drop in. You know what he is.

Jimmy Well, I hope he doesn't. I don't think I could take

Webster tonight.

Alison I thought you said he was the only person who spoke your language.

Jimmy So he is. Different dialect but same language. I like him. He's got bite, edge, drive –

Alison Enthusiasm.

Jimmy You've got it. When he comes here, I begin to feel exhilarated. He doesn't like me, but he gives me something, which is more than I get from most people. Not since –

Alison Yes, we know. Not since you were living with Madeline.

She folds some of the clothes she has already ironed, and crosses to the bed with them.

Cliff (*behind paper again*) Who's Madeline?

Alison Oh, wake up, dear. You've heard about Madeline enough times. She was his mistress. Remember? When he was fourteen. Or was it thirteen?

Jimmy Eighteen.

Alison He owes just about everything to Madeline.

Cliff I get mixed up with all your women. Was she the one all those years older than you?

Jimmy Ten years.

Cliff Proper little Marchbanks, you are!

Jimmy What time's that concert on? (*checks paper*)

Cliff (*yawns*) Oh, I feel so sleepy. Don't feel like standing behind that blinking sweet-stall again tomorrow. Why don't you do it on your own, and let me sleep in?

Jimmy I've got to be at the factory first thing, to get some more stock, so you'll have to put it up on your own. Another five minutes.

Alison has returned to her ironing board. She stands with her arms folded, smoking, staring thoughtfully.

She had more animation in her little finger than you two put together.

Cliff Who did?

Alison Madeline.

Jimmy Her curiosity about things, and about people was staggering. It wasn't just a naïve nosiness. With her, it was simply the delight of being awake, and watching.

Alison starts to press Cliff's trousers.

Cliff (*behind paper*) Perhaps I will make some tea, after all.

Jimmy (*quietly*) Just to be with her was an adventure. Even to sit on the top of a bus with her was like setting out with Ulysses.

Cliff Wouldn't have said Webster was much like Ulysses. He's an ugly little devil.

Jimmy I'm not talking about Webster, stupid. He's all right though, in his way. A sort of female Emily Brontë. He's the only one of your friends (*to Alison*) who's worth tuppence, anyway. I'm surprised you get on with him.

Alison So is he, I think.

Jimmy (*rising to window R, and looking out*) He's not only got guts, but sensitivity as well. That's about the rarest combination I can think of. None of your other friends has got either.

Alison (*very quietly and earnestly*) Jimmy, please – don't go on.

He turns and looks at her. The tired appeal in her voice has pulled him up suddenly. But he soon gathers himself for a new assault. He walks C, behind Cliff, and stands, looking down at his head.

Jimmy Your friends – there's a shower for you.

Cliff (*mumbling*) Dry up. Let her get on with my trousers.

Jimmy (*musingly*) Don't think I could provoke her. Nothing I could do would provoke her. Not even if I were to drop dead.

Cliff Then drop dead.

Jimmy They're either militant like her Mummy and Daddy. Militant, arrogant and full of malice. Or vague. She's somewhere between the two.

Cliff Why don't you listen to that concert of yours? And don't stand behind me. That blooming droning on behind me gives me a funny feeling down the spine.

Jimmy gives his ears a twist and Cliff roars with pain. Jimmy grins back at him.

That hurt, you rotten sadist! (*to Alison*) I wish you'd kick his head in for him.

Jimmy (*moving in between them*) Have you ever seen her brother? Brother Nigel? The straight-backed, chinless wonder from Sandhurst? I only met him once myself. He asked me to step outside when I told his mother she was evil minded.

Cliff And did you?

Jimmy Certainly not. He's a big chap. Well, you've never heard so many well-bred commonplaces come from beneath the same bowler hat. The Platitude from Outer Space – that's brother Nigel. He'll end up in the Cabinet one day, make no mistake. But somewhere at the back of that mind is the vague knowledge that he and his pals have been plundering and

14

fooling everybody for generations. (*going upstage, and turning*) Now Nigel is just about as vague as you can get without being actually invisible. And invisible politicians aren't much use to anyone – not even to *his* supporters! And nothing is more vague about Nigel than his knowledge. His knowledge of life and ordinary human beings is so hazy, he really deserves some sort of decoration for it – a medal inscribed 'For Vaguery in the Field'. But it wouldn't do for him to be troubled by any stabs of conscience, however vague. (*moving down again*) Besides, he's a patriot and an Englishman, and he doesn't like the idea that he may have been selling out his countryman all these years, so what does he do? The only thing he *can* do – seek sanctuary in his own stupidity. The only way to keep things as much like they always have been as possible, is to make any alternative too much for your poor, tiny brain to grasp. It takes some doing nowadays. It really does. But they knew all about character building at Nigel's school, and he'll make it all right. Don't you worry, he'll make it. And, what's more, he'll do it better than anybody else!

There is no sound, only the plod of Alison's iron. Her eyes are fixed on what she is doing. Cliff stares at the floor. His cheerfulness has deserted him for the moment. Jimmy is rather shakily triumphant. He cannot allow himself to look at either of them to catch their responses to his rhetoric, so he moves across to the window, to recover himself, and look out.

It's started to rain. That's all it needs. This room and the rain.

He's been cheated out of his response, but he's got to draw blood somehow.

(*conversationally*) Yes, that's the little woman's family. You know Mummy and Daddy, of course. And don't let the Marquess of Queensbury manner fool you. They'll kick you in the groin while you're handing your hat to the maid. As for Nigel and Alison – (*in a reverent, Stuart Hibberd voice*) Nigel and Alison. They're what they sound like: sycophantic, phlegmatic and pusillanimous.

Cliff I'll bet the concert's started by now. Shall I put it on?

Jimmy I looked up that word the other day. It's one of those words I've never been quite sure of, but always thought I knew.

Cliff What was that?

Jimmy I told you – pusillanimous. Do you know what it means?

Cliff shakes his head.

Neither did I really. All this time, I have been married to this woman, this monument to non-attachment, and suddenly I discover that there is actually a word that sums her up. Not just an adjective in the English language to describe her with – it's her name! Pusillanimous! It sounds like some fleshy Roman matron, doesn't it? The Lady Pusillanimous seen here with her husband Sextus, on their way to the Games.

Cliff looks troubled, and glances uneasily at Alison.

Poor old Sextus! If he were put into a Hollywood film, he's so unimpressive, they'd make some poor British actor play the part. He doesn't know it, but those beefcake Christians will make off with his wife in the wonder of stereophonic sound before the picture's over.

Alison leans against the board, and closes her eyes.

The Lady Pusillanimous has been promised a brighter easier world than old Sextus can ever offer her. Hi, Pusey! What say we get the hell down to the Arena, and maybe feed ourselves to a couple of lions, huh?

Alison God help me, if he doesn't stop, I'll go out of my mind in a minute.

16

Jimmy Why don't you? That would be something, anyway. (*crosses to chest of drawers R*) But I haven't told you what it means yet, have I? (*picks up dictionary*) I don't have to tell her – she knows. In fact, if my pronunciation is at fault, she'll probably wait for a suitably public moment to correct it. Here it is. I quote: Pusillanimous. Adjective. Wanting of firmness of mind, of small courage, having a little mind, mean spirited, cowardly, timid of mind. From the Latin pusillus, very little, and animus, the mind. (*slams the book shut*) That's my wife! That's *her* isn't it? Behold the Lady Pusillanimous. (*shouting hoarsely*) Hi, Pusey! When's your next picture?

Jimmy watches her, waiting for her to break. For no more than a flash, Alison's face seems to contort, and it looks as though she might throw her head back, and scream. But it passes in a moment. She is used to these carefully rehearsed attacks, and it doesn't look as though he will get his triumph tonight. She carries on with her ironing. Jimmy crosses, and switches on the radio. The Vaughan Williams concert has started. He goes back to his chair, leans back in it, and closes his eyes.

Alison (*handing Cliff his trousers*) There you are, dear. They're not very good, but they'll do for now.

Cliff gets up and puts them on.

Cliff Oh, that's lovely.

Alison Now try and look after them. I'll give them a real press later on.

Cliff Thank you, you beautiful, darling girl.

He puts his arms around her waist, and kisses her. She smiles, and gives his nose a tug. Jimmy watches from his chair.

Alison (*to Cliff*) Let's have a cigarette, shall we?

Cliff That's a good idea. Where are they?

Alison On the stove. Do you want one Jimmy?

Jimmy No thank you, I'm trying to listen. Do you mind?

Cliff Sorry, your lordship.

He puts a cigarette in Alison's mouth, and one in his own, and lights up. Cliff sits down, and picks up his paper. Alison goes back to her board. Cliff throws down paper, picks up another, and thumbs through that.

Jimmy Do you have to make all that racket?

Cliff Oh, sorry.

Jimmy It's quite a simple thing, you know – turning over a page. Anyway, that's my paper. (*snatches it away*)

Cliff Oh, don't be so mean!

Jimmy Price ninepence, obtainable from any newsagent's. Now let me hear the music, for God's sake.

Pause.

(*to Alison*) Are you going to be much longer doing that?

Alison Why?

Jimmy Perhaps you haven't noticed it, but it's interfering with the radio.

Alison I'm sorry. I shan't be much longer.

A pause. The iron mingles with the music. Cliff shifts restlessly in his chair. Jimmy watches Alison, his foot beginning to twitch dangerously. Presently, he gets up quickly, crossing below Alison to the radio, and turns it off.

What did you do that for?

Jimmy I wanted to listen to the concert, that's all.

Alison Well, what's stopping you?

Jimmy Everyone's making such a din – that's what's stopping me.

Alison Well, I'm very sorry, but I can't just stop everything because you want to listen to music.

Jimmy Why not?

Alison Really, Jimmy, you're like a child.

Jimmy Don't try and patronize me. (*turning to Cliff*) She's so clumsy. I watch for her to do the same things every night. The way she jumps on the bed, as if she were stamping on someone's face, and draws the curtains back with a great clatter, in that casually destructive way of hers. It's like someone launching a battleship. Have you ever noticed how noisy women are? (*crosses below chairs to LC*) Have you? The way they kick the floor about, simply walking over it? Or have you watched them sitting at their dressing tables, dropping their weapons and banging down their bits of boxes and brushes and lipsticks?

He faces her dressing table.

I've watched her doing it night after night. When you see a woman in front of her bedroom mirror, you realize what a refined sort of a butcher she is. (*turns in*) Did you ever see some dirty old Arab, sticking his fingers into some mess of lamb fat and gristle? Well, she's just like that. Thank God they don't have many women surgeons! Those primitive hands would have your guts out in no time. Flip! Out it comes, like the powder out of its box. Flop! Back it goes, like the powder puff on the table.

Cliff (*grimacing cheerfully*) Ugh! Stop it!

Jimmy (*moving upstage*) She'd drop your guts like hair clips

19

and fluff all over the floor. You've got to be fundamentally insensitive to be as noisy and as clumsy as that.

He moves C, and leans against the table.

I had a flat underneath a couple of girls once. You heard every damned thing those bastards did, all day and night. The most simple, everyday actions were a sort of assault course on your sensibilities. I used to plead with them. I even got to screaming the most ingenious obscenities I could think of, up the stairs at them. But nothing, nothing, would move them. With those two, even a simple visit to the lavatory sounded like a medieval siege. Oh, they beat me in the end – I had to go. I expect they're still at it. Or they're probably married by now, and driving some other poor devils out of their minds. Slamming their doors, stamping their high heels, banging their irons and saucepans – the eternal flaming racket of the female.

Church bells start ringing outside.

Oh, hell! Now the bloody bells have started! (*He rushes to the window.*) Wrap it up, will you? Stop ringing those bells! There's somebody going crazy in here! I don't want to hear them!

Alison Stop shouting! (*recovering immediately*) You'll have Miss Drury up here.

Jimmy I don't give a damn about Miss Drury – that mild old gentlewoman doesn't fool me, even if she takes in you two. She's an old robber. She gets more than enough out of us for this place every week. Anyway, she's probably in church, (*points to the window*) swinging on those bloody bells!

Cliff goes to the window, and closes it.

Cliff Come on now, be a good boy. I'll take us all out, and we'll have a drink.

Jimmy They're not open yet. It's Sunday. Remember? Anyway, it's raining.

Cliff Well, shall we dance?

He pushes Jimmy round the floor, who is past the mood for this kind of fooling.

Do you come here often?

Jimmy Only in the mating season. All right, all right, very funny.

He tries to escape, but Cliff holds him like a vice.

Let me go.

Cliff Not until you've apologized for being nasty to everyone. Do you think bosoms will be in or out, this year?

Jimmy Your teeth will be out in a minute, if you don't let go!

He makes a great effort to wrench himself free, but Cliff hangs on. They collapse to the floor C, below the table, struggling. Alison carries on with her ironing. This is routine, but she is getting close to breaking point, all the same. Cliff manages to break away, and finds himself in front of the ironing board. Jimmy springs up. They grapple.

Alison Look out, for heaven's sake! Oh, it's more like a zoo every day!

Jimmy makes a frantic, deliberate effort, and manages to push Cliff on to the ironing board, and into Alison. The board collapses. Cliff falls against her, and they end up in a heap on the floor. Alison cries out in pain. Jimmy looks down at them, dazed and breathless.

Cliff (*picking himself up*) She's hurt. Are you all right?

Alison Well, does it look like it!

Cliff She's burnt her arm on the iron.

Jimmy Darling, I'm sorry.

Alison Get out!

Jimmy I'm sorry, believe me. You think I did it on pur –

Alison (*her head shaking helplessly*) Clear out of my *sight*!

He stares at her uncertainly. Cliff nods to him, and he turns and goes out of the door.

Cliff Come and sit down.

He leads her to the armchair. R.

You look a bit white. Are you all right?

Alison Yes. I'm all right now.

Cliff Let's have a look at your arm. (*examines it*) Yes, it's quite red. That's going to be painful. What should I do with it?

Alison Oh, it's nothing much. A bit of soap on it will do. I never can remember what you do with burns.

Cliff I'll just pop down to the bathroom and get some. Are you sure you're all right?

Alison Yes.

Cliff (*crossing to door*) Won't be a minute. (*He exits.*)

She leans back in the chair, and looks up at the ceiling. She breathes in deeply, and brings her hands up to her face. She winces as she feels the pain in her arm, and she lets it fall. She runs her hand through her hair.

Alison (*in a clenched whisper*) Oh, God!

Cliff re-enters with a bar of soap.

Cliff It's this scented muck. Do you think it'll be all right?

22

Alison That'll do.

Cliff Here we are then. Let's have your arm.

He kneels down beside her, and she holds out her arm.

I've put it under the tap. It's quite soft. I'll do it ever so gently.

Very carefully, he rubs the soap over the burn.

All right? (*She nods.*) You're a brave girl.

Alison I don't feel very brave. (*tears harshening her voice*) I really don't, Cliff. I don't think I can take much more. (*turns her head away*) I think I feel rather sick.

Cliff All over now. (*puts the soap down*) Would you like me to get you something?

She shakes her head. He sits on the arm of the chair, and puts his arm round her. She leans her head back on to him.

Don't upset yourself, lovely.

He massages the back of her neck, and she lets her head fall forward.

Alison Where is he?

Cliff In my room.

Alison What's he doing?

Cliff Lying on the bed. Reading, I think. (*stroking her neck*) That better?

She leans back, and closes her eyes again.

Alison Bless you.

He kisses the top of her head.

Cliff I don't think I'd have the courage to live on my own again – in spite of everything. I'm pretty rough, and pretty ordinary really, and I'd seem worse on my own. And you get fond of people too, worse luck.

Alison I don't think I want anything more to do with love. Any more. I can't take it on.

Cliff You're too young to start giving up. Too young, and too lovely. Perhaps I'd better put a bandage on that – do you think so?

Alison There's some on my dressing table.

Cliff crosses to the dressing table R.

I keep looking back, as far as I remember, and I can't think what it was to feel young, really young. Jimmy said the same thing to me the other day. I pretended not to be listening – because I knew that would hurt him, I suppose. And – of course – he got savage, like tonight. But I knew just what he meant. I suppose it would have been so easy to say 'Yes, darling, I know just what you mean. I know what you're feeling.' (*shrugs*) It's those easy things that seem to be so impossible with us.

Cliff stands down R, holding the bandage, his back to her.

Cliff I'm wondering how much longer I can go on watching you two tearing the insides out of each other. It looks pretty ugly sometimes.

Alison You wouldn't seriously think of leaving us, would you?

Cliff I suppose not. (*crosses to her*)

Alison I think I'm frightened. If only I knew what was going to happen.

Cliff (*kneeling on the arm of her chair*) Give it here. (*She holds out her arm.*) Yell out if I hurt you. (*He bandages it for her.*)

24

Alison (*staring at her outstretched arm*) Cliff –

Cliff Um? (*slight pause*) What is it, lovely?

Alison Nothing.

Cliff I said: what is it?

Alison You see – (*hesitates*) I'm pregnant.

Cliff (*after a few moments*) I'll need some scissors.

Alison They're over there.

Cliff (*crossing to the dressing table*) That is something, isn't it? When did you find this out?

Alison Few days ago. It was a bit of a shock.

Cliff Yes, I dare say.

Alison After three years of married life, I have to get caught out now.

Cliff None of us infallible, I suppose. (*crosses to her*) Must say I'm surprised though.

Alison It's always been out of the question. What with – this place, and no money, and oh – everything. He's resented it, I know. What can you do?

Cliff You haven't told him yet.

Alison Not yet.

Cliff What are you going to do?

Alison I've no idea.

Cliff (*having cut her bandage, he starts tying it*) That too tight?

Alison Fine, thank you. (*She rises, goes to the ironing board, folds it up, and leans it against the food cupboard R.*)

Cliff Is it . . . Is it . . . ?

Alison Too late to avert the situation? (*places the iron on the rack of the stove*) I'm not certain yet. Maybe not. If not, there won't be any problem, will there?

Cliff And if it is too late?

Her face is turned away from him. She simply shakes her head.

Why don't you tell him now?

She kneels down to pick up the clothes on the floor, and folds them up.

After all, he does love you. You don't need me to tell you that.

Alison Can't you see? He'll suspect my motives at once. He never stops telling himself that I know how vulnerable he is. Tonight it might be all right – we'd make love. But later, we'd both lie awake, watching for the light to come through that little window, and dreading it. In the morning, he'd feel hoaxed, as if I were trying to kill him in the worst way of all. He'd watch me growing bigger every day, and I wouldn't dare to look at him.

Cliff You may have to face it, lovely.

Alison Jimmy's got his own private morality, as you know. What my mother calls 'loose'. It is pretty free, of course, but it's very harsh too. You know, it's funny, but we never slept together before we were married.

Cliff It certainly is – knowing him!

Alison We knew each other such a short time, everything moved at such a pace, we didn't have much opportunity. And, afterwards, he actually taunted me with my virginity. He was quite angry about it, as if I had deceived him in some strange way. He seemed to think an untouched woman would defile him.

Cliff I've never heard you talking like this about him. He'd be quite pleased.

Alison Yes, he would. (*She gets up, the clothes folded over her arm.*) Do you think he's right?

Cliff What about?

Alison Oh – everything.

Cliff Well, I suppose he and I think the same about a lot of things, because we're alike in some ways. We both come from working people, if you like. Oh I know some of his mother's relatives are pretty posh, but he hates them as much as he hates yours. Don't quite know why. Anyway, he gets on with me because I'm common. (*grins*) Common as dirt, that's me.

She puts her hand on his head, and strokes it thoughtfully.

Alison You think I should tell him about the baby?

He gets up, and puts his arm around her.

Cliff It'll be all right – you see. Tell him.

He kisses her. Enter Jimmy. He looks at them curiously, but without surprise. They are both aware of him, but make no sign of it. He crosses to the armchair L, and sits down next to them. He picks up a paper, and starts looking at it. Cliff glances at him, Alison's head against his cheek.

There you are, you old devil, you! Where have you been?

Jimmy You know damn well where I've been. (*without looking at her*) How's your arm?

Alison Oh, it's all right. It wasn't much.

Cliff She's beautiful, isn't she?

Jimmy You seem to think so.

Cliff and Alison still have their arms round one another.

Cliff Why the hell she married you, I'll never know.

Jimmy You think she'd have been better off with you?

Cliff I'm not her type. Am I, dullin'?

Alison I'm not sure what my type is.

Jimmy Why don't you both get into bed, and have done with it.

Alison You know, I think he really means that.

Jimmy I do. I can't concentrate with you two standing there like that.

Cliff He's just an old Puritan at heart.

Jimmy Perhaps I am, at that. Anyway, you both look pretty silly slobbering over each other.

Cliff I think she's beautiful. And so do you, only you're too much of a pig to say so.

Jimmy You're just a sexy little Welshman, and you know it! Mummy and Daddy turn pale, and face the east every time they remember she's married to me. But if they saw all this going on, they'd collapse. Wonder what they would do, incidentally. Send for the police I expect. (*genuinely friendly*) Have you got a cigarette?

Alison (*disengaging*) I'll have a look. (*She goes to her handbag on the table C.*)

Jimmy (*pointing at Cliff*) He gets more like a little mouse every day, doesn't he?

He is trying to re-establish himself.

He really does look like one. Look at those ears, and that face, and the little short legs.

Alison (*looking through her bag*) That's because he *is* a mouse.

Cliff Eek! Eek! I'm a mouse.

Jimmy A randy little mouse.

Cliff (*dancing round the table, and squeaking*) I'm a mouse, I'm a mouse, I'm a randy little mouse. That's a mourris dance.

Jimmy A what?

Cliff A *Mourris Dance*. That's a Morris Dance strictly for mice.

Jimmy You stink. You really do. Do you know that?

Cliff Not as bad as you, you horrible old bear. (*goes over to him, and grabs his foot*) You're a stinking old bear, you hear me?

Jimmy Let go of my foot, you whimsy little half-wit. You're making my stomach heave. I'm resting! If you don't let go, I'll cut off your nasty, great, slimy tail!

Cliff gives him a tug, and Jimmy falls to the floor. Alison watches them, relieved and suddenly full of affection.

Alison I've run out of cigarettes.

Cliff is dragging Jimmy along the floor by his feet.

Jimmy (*yelling*) Go out and get me some cigarettes, and stop playing the fool!

Cliff OK.

He lets go of Jimmy's legs suddenly, who yells again as his head bangs on the floor.

Alison Here's half a crown. (*giving it him*) The shop on the corner will be open.

Cliff Right you are. (*kisses her on the forehead quickly*) Don't forget. (*crosses upstage to door*)

Jimmy Now get the hell out of here!

Cliff (*at door*) Hey, shorty!

Jimmy What do you want?

Cliff Make a nice pot of tea.

Jimmy (*getting up*) I'll kill you first.

Cliff (*grinning*) That's my boy! (*He exits.*)

Jimmy is now beside Alison, who is still looking through her handbag. She becomes aware of his nearness, and, after a few moments, closes it. He takes hold of her bandaged arm.

Jimmy How's it feeling?

Alison Fine. It wasn't anything.

Jimmy All this fooling about can get a bit dangerous.

He sits on the edge of the table, holding her hand.

I'm sorry.

Alison I know.

Jimmy I mean it.

Alison There's no need.

Jimmy I did it on purpose.

Alison Yes.

Jimmy There's hardly a moment when I'm not – watching and wanting you. I've got to hit out somehow. Nearly four years of being in the same room with you, night and day, and I still can't stop my sweat breaking out when I see you doing – something as ordinary as leaning over an ironing board.

She strokes his head, not sure of herself yet.

(*sighing*) Trouble is – Trouble is you get used to people. Even their trivialities become indispensable to you. Indispensable, and a little mysterious.

He slides his head forward, against her, trying to catch his thoughts.

I think . . . I must have a lot of – old stock . . . Nobody wants it . . .

He puts his face against her belly. She goes on stroking his head, still on guard a little. Then he lifts his head, and they kiss passionately.

What are we going to do tonight?

Alison What would you like to do? Drink?

Jimmy I know what I want now.

She takes his head in her hands and kisses him.

Alison Well, you'll have to wait till the proper time.

Jimmy There's no such thing.

Alison Cliff will be back in a minute.

Jimmy What did he mean by 'don't forget'?

Alison Something I've been meaning to tell you.

Jimmy (*kissing her again*) You're fond of him, aren't you?

Alison Yes, I am.

Jimmy He's the only friend I seem to have left now. People go away. You never see them again. I can remember lots of names – men and women. When I was at school – Watson, Roberts, Davies. Jenny, Madeline, Hugh . . . (*pause*) And there's Hugh's mum, of course. I'd almost forgotten her. She's been a good friend to us, if you like. She's even letting me buy the sweet-stall off her in my own time. She only bought it for us, anyway. She's so fond of you. I can never understand why you're so – distant with her.

Alison (*alarmed at this threat of a different mood*) Jimmy – please no!

Jimmy (*staring at her anxious face*) You're very beautiful. A beautiful, great-eyed squirrel.

She nods brightly, relieved.

Hoarding, nut-munching squirrel. (*She mimes this delightedly.*) With highly polished, gleaming fur, and an ostrich feather of a tail.

Alison Wheeeeeeeeeee!

Jimmy How I envy you.

He stands, her arms around his neck.

Alison Well, you're a jolly super bear, too. A really soooooooooooooooooper, marvellous bear.

Jimmy Bears and squirrels *are* marvellous.

Alison Marvellous *and* beautiful. (*She jumps up and down excitedly, making little 'paw gestures'.*) Oooooooooh! Ooooooooooh!

Jimmy What the hell's that?

Alison That's a dance squirrels do when they're happy.

They embrace again.

Jimmy What makes you think you're happy?

Alison Everything just seems all right suddenly. That's all. Jimmy –

Jimmy Yes?

Alison You know I told you I'd something to tell you?

Jimmy Well?

Cliff appears in the doorway.

Cliff Didn't get any further than the front door. Miss Drury hadn't gone to church after all. I couldn't get away from her. (*to Alison*) Someone on the phone for you.

Alison On the phone? Who on earth is it?

Cliff Helena something.

Jimmy and Alison look at each other quickly.

Jimmy (*to Cliff*) Helena Charles?

Cliff That's it.

Alison Thank you, Cliff. (*moves upstage*) I won't be a minute.

Cliff You will. Old Miss Drury will keep you down there for ever. She doesn't think we keep this place clean enough. (*comes and sits in the armchair down R*) Thought you were going to make me some tea, you rotter.

Jimmy makes no reply.

What's the matter, boyo?

Jimmy (*slowly*) That bitch.

Cliff Who?

Jimmy (*to himself*) Helena Charles.

Cliff Who is this Helena?

Jimmy One of her old friends. And one of my natural

enemies. You're sitting on my chair.

Cliff Where are we going for a drink?

Jimmy I don't know.

Cliff Well, you were all for it earlier on.

Jimmy What does she want? What would make her ring up?
It can't be for anything pleasant. Oh well, we shall soon
know. (*He settles on the table.*) Few minutes ago things didn't
seem so bad either. I've just about had enough of this
'expense of spirit' lark, as far as women are concerned.
Honestly, it's enough to make you become a scoutmaster or
something isn't it? Sometimes I almost envy old Gide and the
Greek Chorus boys. Oh, I'm not saying that it mustn't be hell
for them a lot of the time. But, at least, they do seem to have
a cause – not a particularly good one, it's true. But plenty of
them do seem to have a revolutionary fire about them, which
is more than you can say for the rest of us. Like Webster, for
instance. He doesn't like me – they hardly ever do.

*He is talking for the sake of it, only half listening to what
he is saying.*

I dare say he suspects me because I refuse to treat him either
as a clown or as a tragic hero. He's like a man with a
strawberry mark – he keeps thrusting it in your face because
he can't believe it doesn't interest or horrify you particularly.
(*Picks up Alison's handbag thoughtfully, and starts looking
through it.*) As if I give a damn which way he likes his meat
served up. I've got my own strawberry mark – only it's in a
different place. No, as far as the Michelangelo Brigade's
concerned, I must be a sort of right-wing deviationist. If the
Revolution ever comes, I'll be the first to be put up against
the wall, with all the other poor old liberals.

Cliff (*indicating Alison's handbag*) Wouldn't you say that
that was her private property?

34

Jimmy You're quite right. But do you know something? Living night and day with another human being has made me predatory and suspicious. I know that the only way of finding out exactly what's going on is to catch them when they don't know you're looking. When she goes out, I go through everything – trunks, cases, drawers, bookcase, everything. Why? To see if there is something of me somewhere, a reference to me. I want to know if I'm being betrayed.

Cliff You look for trouble, don't you?

Jimmy Only because I'm pretty certain of finding it. (*He brings out a letter from the handbag.*) Look at that! Oh, I'm such a fool. This is happening every five minutes of the day. She gets letters. (*He holds it up.*) Letters from her mother, letters in which I'm not mentioned at all because my name is a dirty word. And what does she do?

Enter Alison. He turns to look at her.

She writes long letters back to Mummy, and never mentions me at all, because I'm just a dirty word to her too.

He throws the letter down at her feet.

Well, what did your friend want?

Alison She's at the station. She's – coming over.

Jimmy I see. She said 'Can I come over?' And you said 'My husband, Jimmy – if you'll forgive me using such a dirty word, will be delighted to see you. He'll kick your face in!' (*He stands up, unable to sustain his anger, poised on the table.*)

Alison (*quietly*) She's playing with the company at the Hippodrome this week, and she's got no digs. She can't find anywhere to stay –

Jimmy That I don't believe!

Alison So I said she could come here until she fixes

something else. Miss Drury's got a spare room downstairs.

Jimmy Why not have her in here? Did you tell her to bring her armour? Because she's going to need it!

Alison (*vehemently*) Oh why don't you shut up, please!

Jimmy Oh, my dear wife, you've got so much to learn. I only hope you learn it one day. If only something – something would happen to you, and wake you out of your beauty sleep! (*coming in close to her*) If you could have a child, and it would die. Let it grow, let a recognizable human face emerge from that little mass of indiarubber and wrinkles. (*She retreats away from him.*) Please – if only I could watch you face that. I wonder if you might even become a recognizable human being yourself. But I doubt it.

She moves away, stunned, and leans on the gas stove down L. He stands rather helplessly on his own.

Do you know I have never known the great pleasure of lovemaking when I didn't desire it myself. Oh, it's not that she hasn't her own kind of passion. She has the passion of a python. She just devours me whole every time, as if I were some over-large rabbit. That's me. That bulge around her navel – if you're wondering what it is – it's me. Me, buried alive down there, and going mad, smothered in that peaceful looking coil. Not a sound, not a flicker from her – she doesn't even rumble a little. You'd think that this indigestible mess would stir up some kind of tremor in those distended, overfed tripes – but not her! (*crosses up to the door*) She'll go on sleeping and devouring until there's nothing left of me. (*He exits.*)

Alison's head goes back as if she were about to make some sound. But her mouth remains open and trembling, as Cliff looks on.

Act II
SCENE ONE

Two weeks later. Evening.

Alison is standing over the gas stove, pouring water from the kettle into a large teapot. She is only wearing a slip, and her feet are bare. In the room across the hall, Jimmy is playing on his jazz trumpet, in intermittent bursts. Alison takes the pot to the table C, which is laid for four people. The Sunday paper jungle around the two armchairs is as luxuriant as ever. It is late afternoon, the end of a hot day. She wipes her forehead. She crosses to the dressing table R, takes out a pair of stockings from one of the drawers, and sits down on the small chair beside it to put them on. While she is doing this, the door opens and **Helena** *enters. She is the same age as Alison, medium height, carefully and expensively dressed. Now and again, when she allows her rather judicial expression of alertness to soften, she is very attractive. Her sense of matriarchal authority makes most men who meet her anxious, not only to please but impress, as if she were the gracious representative of visiting royalty. In this case, the royalty of that middle-class womanhood, which is so eminently secure in its divine rights, that it can afford to tolerate the parliament, and reasonably free assembly of its menfolk. Even from other young women, like Alison, she receives her due of respect and admiration. In Jimmy, as one would expect, she arouses all the rabble-rousing instincts of his spirit. And she is not accustomed to having to defend herself against catcalls. However, her sense of modestly exalted responsibility enables her to behave with an impressive show of strength and dignity, although the strain of this is beginning to tell on her a little. She is carrying a large salad colander.*

Alison Did you manage all right?

Helena Of course. I've prepared most of the meals in the last week, you know.

Alison Yes, you have. It's been wonderful having someone to help. Another woman, I mean.

Helena (*crossing down L*) I'm enjoying it. Although I don't think I shall ever get used to having to go down to the bathroom every time I want some water for something.

Alison It is primitive, isn't it?

Helena Yes. It is rather. (*She starts tearing up green salad on to four plates, which she takes from the food cupboard.*) Looking after one man is really enough, but two is rather an undertaking.

Alison Oh, Cliff looks after himself, more or less. In fact, he helps me quite a lot.

Helena Can't say I'd noticed it.

Alison You've been doing it instead, I suppose.

Helena I see.

Alison You've settled in so easily somehow.

Helena Why shouldn't I?

Alison It's not exactly what you're used to, is it?

Helena And are you used to it?

Alison Everything seems very different here now – with you here.

Helena Does it?

Alison Yes. I was on my own before –

Helena Now you've got me. So you're not sorry you asked me to stay?

Alison Of course not. Did you tell him his tea was ready?

Helena I banged on the door to Cliff's room, and yelled. He didn't answer, but he must have heard. I don't know where Cliff is.

Alison (*leaning back in her chair*) I thought I'd feel cooler after a bath, but I feel hot again already. God, I wish he'd lose that damned trumpet.

Helena I imagine that's for my benefit.

Alison Miss Drury will ask us to go soon, I know it. Thank goodness she isn't in. Listen to him.

Helena Does he drink?

Alison Drink? (*rather startled*) He's not an alcoholic, if that's what you mean.

They both pause, listening to the trumpet.

He'll have the rest of the street banging on the door next.

Helena (*pondering*) It's almost as if he wanted to kill someone with it. And me in particular. I've never seen such hatred in someone's eyes before. It's slightly horrifying. Horrifying (*crossing to food cupboard for tomatoes, beetroot and cucumber*) and oddly exciting.

Alison faces her dressing mirror, and brushes her hair.

Alison He had his own jazz band once. That was when he was still a student, before I knew him. I rather think he'd like to start another, and give up the stall altogether.

Helena Is Cliff in love with you?

Alison (*stops brushing for a moment*) No . . . I don't think so.

Helena And what about you? You look as though I've asked you a rather peculiar question. The way things are, you might as well be frank with me. I only want to help. After all, your behaviour together is a little strange – by most people's standards, to say the least.

Alison You mean you've seen us embracing each other?

Helena Well, it doesn't seem to go on as much as it did, I admit. Perhaps he finds my presence inhibiting – even if Jimmy's isn't.

Alison We're simply fond of each other – there's no more to it than that.

Helena Darling, really! It can't be as simple as that.

Alison You mean there must be something physical too? I suppose there is, but it's not exactly a consuming passion with either of us. It's just a relaxed, cheerful sort of thing, like being warm in bed. You're too comfortable to bother about moving for the sake of some other pleasure.

Helena I find it difficult to believe anyone's that lazy!

Alison I think *we* are.

Helena And what about Jimmy? After all, he is your husband. Do you mean to say he actually approves of it?

Alison It isn't easy to explain. It's what he would call a question of allegiances, and he expects you to be pretty literal about them. Not only about himself and all the things he believes in, his present and his future, but his past as well. All the people he admires and loves, and has loved. The friends he used to know, people I've never even known – and probably wouldn't have liked. His father, who died years ago. Even the other women he's loved. Do you understand?

Helena Do you?

Alison I've tried to. But I still can't bring myself to feel the way he does about things. I can't believe that he's right somehow.

Helena Well, that's something, anyway.

Alison If things have worked out with Cliff, it's because he's kind and lovable, and I've grown genuinely fond of him. But it's been a fluke. It's worked because Cliff is such a nice person anyway. With Hugh, it was quite different.

Helena Hugh?

Alison Hugh Tanner. He and Jimmy were friends almost from childhood. Mrs Tanner is his mother –

Helena Oh yes – the one who started him off in the sweet business.

Alison That's right. Well, after Jimmy and I were married, we'd no money – about eight pounds ten in actual fact – and no home. He didn't even have a job. He'd only left the university about a year. (*smiles*) No – left. I don't think one 'comes down' from Jimmy's university. According to him, it's not even red brick, but white tile. Anyway, we went off to live in Hugh's flat. It was over a warehouse in Poplar.

Helena Yes. I remember seeing the postmark on your letters.

Alison Well, that was where I found myself on my wedding night. Hugh and I disliked each other on sight, and Jimmy knew it. He was so proud of us both, so pathetically anxious that we should take to each other. Like a child showing off his toys. We had a little wedding celebration, and the three of us tried to get tight on some cheap port they'd brought in. Hugh got more and more subtly insulting – he'd a rare talent for that. Jimmy got steadily depressed, and I just sat there, listening to their talk, looking and feeling very stupid. For the first time in my life, I was cut off from the kind of people I'd always known, my family, my friends, everybody. And I'd burnt my boats. After all those weeks of brawling with Mummy and Daddy about Jimmy, I knew I couldn't appeal to them without looking foolish and cheap. It was just before the General Election, I remember, and Nigel was busy getting himself into Parliament. He didn't have time for anyone but his constituents. Oh, he'd have been sweet and kind, I know.

Helena (*moving in C*) Darling, why didn't you come to me?

Alison You were away on tour in some play, I think.

Helena So I was.

Alison Those next few months at the flat in Poplar were a nightmare. I suppose I must be soft and squeamish, and snobbish, but I felt as though I'd been dropped in a jungle. I couldn't believe that two people, two educated people could be so savage, and so – so uncompromising. Mummy has always said that Jimmy is utterly ruthless, but she hasn't met Hugh. He takes the first prize for ruthlessness – from all comers. Together, they were frightening. They both came to regard me as a sort of hostage from those sections of society they had declared war on.

Helena How were you living all this time?

Alison I had a tiny bit coming in from a few shares I had left, but it hardly kept us. Mummy had made me sign everything else over to her, in trust, when she knew I was really going to marry Jimmy.

Helena Just as well, I imagine.

Alison They soon thought of a way out of that. A brilliant campaign. They started inviting themselves – through me – to people's houses, friends of Nigel's and mine, friends of Daddy's, oh everyone: the Arksdens, the Tarnatts, the Wains –

Helena Not the Wains?

Alison Just about everyone I'd ever known. Your people must have been among the few we missed out. It was just enemy territory to them, and, as I say, they used me as a hostage. We'd set out from headquarters in Poplar, and carry out our raids on the enemy in w1, sw1, sw3 and w8. In my name, we'd gatecrash everywhere – cocktails, week-ends, even a couple of houseparties. I used to hope that one day, somebody would have the guts to slam the door in our faces, but they didn't. They were too well-bred, and probably sorry for me as well. Hugh and Jimmy despised them for it. So we went on plundering them, wolfing their food and drinks, and smoking their cigars like ruffians. Oh, they enjoyed themselves.

Helena Apparently.

Alison Hugh fairly revelled in the role of the barbarian invader. Sometimes I thought he might even dress the part – you know, furs, spiked helmet, sword. He even got a fiver out of old Man Wain once. Blackmail, of course. People would have signed almost anything to get rid of us. He told him that we were about to be turned out of our flat for not paying the rent. At least it was true.

Helena I don't understand you. You must have been crazy.

Alison Afraid more than anything.

Helena But letting them do it! Letting them get away with it! You managed to stop them stealing the silver, I suppose?

Alison Oh, they knew their guerrilla warfare better than that. Hugh tried to seduce some fresh-faced young girl at the Arksdens' once, but that was the only time we were more or less turned out.

Helena It's almost unbelievable. I don't understand your part in it all. Why? That's what I don't see. Why did you –

Alison Marry him? There must be about six different answers. When the family came back from India, everything seemed, I don't know – unsettled? Anyway, Daddy seemed remote and rather irritable. And Mummy – well, you know

Mummy. I didn't have much to worry about. I didn't know I was born as Jimmy says. I met him at a party. I remember it so clearly. I was almost twenty-one. The men there all looked as though they distrusted him, and as for the women, they were all intent on showing their contempt for this rather odd creature, but no one seemed quite sure how to do it. He'd come to the party on a bicycle, he told me, and there was oil all over his dinner jacket. It had been such a lovely day, and he'd been in the sun. Everything about him seemed to burn, his face, the edges of his hair glistened and seemed to spring off his head, and his eyes were so blue and full of the sun. He looked so young and frail, in spite of the tired line of his mouth. I knew I was taking on more than I was ever likely to be capable of bearing, but there never seemed to be any choice. Well, the howl of outrage and astonishment went up from the family, and that did it. Whether or not he was in love with me, that did it. He made up his mind to marry me. They did just about everything they could think of to stop us.

Helena Yes, it wasn't a very pleasant business. But you can see their point.

Alison Jimmy went into battle with his axe swinging round his head – frail, and so full of fire. I had never seen anything like it. The old story of the knight in shining armour – except that his armour didn't really shine very much.

Helena And what about Hugh?

Alison Things got steadily worse between us. He and Jimmy even went to some of Nigel's political meetings. They took bunches of their Poplar cronies with them, and broke them up for him.

Helena He's really a savage, isn't he?

Alison Well, Hugh was writing some novel or other, and he made up his mind he must go abroad – to China, or some God-forsaken place. He said that England was finished for

44

us, anyway. All the old gang was back – Dame Alison's Mob, as he used to call it. The only real hope was to get out, and try somewhere else. He wanted us to go with him, but Jimmy refused to go. There was a terrible, bitter row over it. Jimmy accused Hugh of giving up, and he thought it was wrong of him to go off for ever, and leave his mother all on her own. He was upset by the whole idea. They quarrelled for days over it. I almost wished they'd both go, and leave me behind. Anyway, they broke up. A few months later we came up here, and Hugh went off to find the New Millennium on his own. Sometimes, I think Hugh's mother blames me for it all. Jimmy too, in a way, although he's never said so. He never mentions it. But whenever that woman looks at me, I can feel her thinking 'If it hadn't been for you, everything would have been all right. We'd have all been happy.' Not that I dislike her – I don't. She's very sweet, in fact. Jimmy seems to adore her principally because she's been poor almost all her life, and she's frankly ignorant. I'm quite aware how snobbish that sounds, but it happens to be the truth.

Helena Alison, listen to me. You've got to make up your mind what you're going to do. You're going to have a baby, and you have a new responsibility. Before, it was different – there was only yourself at stake. But you can't go on living in this way any longer. (*to her*)

Alison I'm so tired. I dread him coming into the room.

Helena Why haven't you told him you're going to have a child?

Alison I don't know. (*suddenly anticipating Helena's train of thought*) Oh, it's his all right. There couldn't be any doubt of that. You see – (*she smiles*) I've never really wanted anyone else.

Helena Listen, darling – you've got to tell him. Either he learns to behave like anyone else, and looks after you –

Alison Or?

Helena Or you must get out of this mad-house. (*trumpet crescendo*) This menagerie. He doesn't seem to know what love or anything else means.

Alison (*pointing to chest of drawers up R*) You see that bear, and that squirrel? Well, that's him, and that's me.

Helena Meaning?

Alison The game we play: bears and squirrels, squirrels and bears.

Helena looks rather blank.

Yes, it's quite mad, I know. Quite mad. (*Picks up the two animals.*) That's him . . . And that's me . . .

Helena I didn't realize he was a bit fey, as well as everything else!

Alison Oh, there's nothing fey about Jimmy. It's just all we seem to have left. Or had left. Even bears and squirrels seem to have gone their own ways now.

Helena Since I arrived?

Alison It started during those first months we had alone together – after Hugh went abroad. It was the one way of escaping from everything – a sort of unholy priesthole of being animals to one another. We could become little furry creatures with little furry brains. Full of dumb, uncomplicated affection for each other. Playful, careless creatures in their own cosy zoo for two. A silly symphony for people who couldn't bear the pain of being human beings any longer. And now, even they are dead, poor little silly animals. They were all love, and no brains. (*She puts them back.*)

Helena (*gripping her arm*) Listen to me. You've got to fight him. Fight, or get out. Otherwise, he *will* kill you.

Enter Cliff.

Cliff There you are, dullin'. Hullo, Helena. Tea ready?

Alison Yes, dear, it's all ready. Give Jimmy a call, will you?

Cliff Right. (*yelling back through door*) Hey, you horrible man! Stop that bloody noise, and come and get your tea! (*coming in C*) Going out?

Helena (*crossing to L*) Yes.

Cliff Pictures?

Helena No. (*pause*) Church.

Cliff (*really surprised*) Oh! I see. Both of you?

Helena Yes. Are you coming?

Cliff Well . . . I – I haven't read the papers properly yet. Tea, tea, tea! Let's have some tea, shall we?

He sits at the upstage end of the table. Helena puts the four plates of salad on it, sits down L, and they begin the meal. Alison is making up her face at her dressing table. Presently, Jimmy enters. He places his trumpet on the bookcase, and comes above the table.

Hullo, boyo. Come and have your tea. That blinkin' trumpet – why don't you stuff it away somewhere?

Jimmy You like it all right. Anyone who doesn't like real jazz, hasn't any feeling either for music or people. (*He sits R end of table.*)

Helena Rubbish.

Jimmy (*to Cliff*) That seems to prove my point for you. Did you know that Webster played the banjo?

Cliff No, does he really?

Helena He said he'd bring it along next time he came.

Alison (*muttering*) Oh, no!

Jimmy Why is it that nobody knows how to treat the papers in this place? Look at them. I haven't even glanced at them yet – not the posh ones, anyway.

Cliff By the way, can I look at your *New* –

Jimmy No, you can't! (*loudly*) You want anything, you pay for it. Like I have to. Price –

Cliff Price ninepence, obtainable from any bookstall! You're a mean old man, that's what you are.

Jimmy What do you want to read it for, anyway? You've no intellect, no curiosity. It all just washes over you. Am I right?

Cliff Right.

Jimmy What are you, you Welsh trash?

Cliff Nothing, that's what I am.

Jimmy Nothing are you? Blimey you ought to be Prime Minister. You must have been talking to some of my wife's friends. They're a very intellectual set, aren't they? I've seen 'em.

Cliff and Helena carry on with their meal.

They all sit around feeling very spiritual, with their mental hands on each other's knees, discussing sex as if it were the Art of Fugue. If you don't want to be an emotional old spinster, just you listen to your dad!

He starts eating. The silent hostility of the two women has set him off on the scent, and he looks quite cheerful, although the occasional, thick edge of his voice belies it.

You know your trouble, son? Too anxious to please.

Helena Thank heavens somebody is!

Jimmy You'll end up like one of those chocolate meringues my wife is so fond of. My wife – that's the one on the tom-toms behind me. Sweet and sticky on the outside, and sink your teeth in it, (*savouring every word*) inside, all white, messy and disgusting. (*offering teapot sweetly to Helena*) Tea?

Helena Thank you.

He smiles, and pours out a cup for her.

Jimmy That's how you'll end up, my boy – black hearted, evil minded and vicious.

Helena (*taking cup*) Thank you.

Jimmy And those old favourites, your friends and mine: sycophantic, phlegmatic, and, of course, top of the bill – pusillanimous.

Helena (*to Alison*) Aren't you going to have your tea?

Alison Won't be long.

Jimmy Thought of the title for a new song today. It's called 'You can quit hanging round my counter Mildred 'cos you'll find my position is closed'. (*turning to Alison suddenly*) Good?

Alison Oh, very good.

Jimmy Thought you'd like it. If I can slip in a religious angle, it should be a big hit. (*to Helena*) Don't you think so? I was thinking you might help me there. (*She doesn't reply.*) It might help you if I recite the lyrics. Let's see now, it's something like this:

I'm so tired of necking,
of pecking, home wrecking,
of empty bed blues –
just pass me the booze.

I'm tired of being hetero
Rather ride on the metero
Just pass me the booze.
This perpetual whoring
Gets quite dull and boring
So avoid that old python coil
And pass me the celibate oil.
You can quit etc.

No?

Cliff Very good, boyo.

Jimmy Oh, yes, and I know what I meant to tell you – I wrote a poem while I was at the market yesterday. If you're interested, which you obviously are. (*to Helena*) It should appeal to you, in particular. It's soaked in the theology of Dante, with a good slosh of Eliot as well. It starts off 'There are no dry cleaners in Cambodia!'

Cliff What do you call it?

Jimmy 'The Cess Pool'. Myself being a stone dropped in it, you see –

Cliff You should be dropped in it, all right.

Helena (*to Jimmy*) Why do you try so hard to be unpleasant?

He turns very deliberately, delighted that she should rise to the bait so soon – he's scarcely in his stride yet.

Jimmy What's that?

Helena Do you have to be so offensive?

Jimmy You mean now? You think I'm being offensive? You underestimate me. (*turning to Alison*) Doesn't she?

Helena I think you're a very tiresome young man.

A slight pause as his delight catches up with him. He roars with laughter.

Jimmy Oh dear, oh dear! My wife's friends! Pass Lady Bracknell the cucumber sandwiches, will you?

He returns to his meal, but his curiosity about Alison's preparation at the mirror won't be denied any longer. He turns round casually, and speaks to her.

Going out?

Alison That's right.

Jimmy On a Sunday evening in this town? Where on earth are you going?

Alison (*rising*) I'm going out with Helena.

Jimmy That's not a direction – that's an affliction.

She crosses to the table, and sits down C. He leans forwards, and addresses her again.

I didn't ask you what was the matter with you. I asked you where you were going.

Helena (*steadily*) She's going to church.

He has been prepared for some plot, but he is as genuinely surprised by this as Cliff was a few minutes earlier.

Jimmy You're doing what?

Silence.

Have you gone out of your mind or something? (*to Helena*) You're determined to win her, aren't you? So it's come to this now! How feeble can you get? (*His rage mounting within.*) When I think of what I did, what I endured, to get you out –

Alison (*recognizing an onslaught on the way, starts to panic*) Oh yes, we all know what you did for me! You rescued me from the wicked clutches of my family, and all my friends! I'd still be rotting away at home, if you hadn't ridden up on your charger, and carried me off!

The wild note in her voice has reassured him. His anger cools and hardens. His voice is quite calm when he speaks.

Jimmy The funny thing is, you know, I really did have to ride up on a white charger – off white, really. Mummy locked her up in their eight bedroomed castle, didn't she? There is no limit to what the middle-aged mummy will do in the holy crusade against ruffians like me. Mummy and I took one quick look at each other, and, from then on, the age of chivalry was dead. I knew that, to protect her innocent young, she wouldn't hesitate to cheat, lie, bully and blackmail. Threatened with me, a young man without money, background or even looks, she'd bellow like a rhinoceros in labour – enough to make every male rhino for miles turn white, and pledge himself to celibacy. But even I underestimated her strength. Mummy may look over-fed and a bit flabby on the outside, but don't let that well-bred guzzler fool you. Underneath all that, she's armour plated – (*He clutches wildly for something to shock Helena with.*) She's as rough as a night in a Bombay brothel, and as tough as a matelot's arm. She's probably in that bloody cistern, taking down every word we say. (*kicks cistern*) Can you 'ear me, mother. (*sits on it, beats like bongo drums*) Just about get her in there. Let me give you an example of this lady's tactics. You may have noticed that I happen to wear my hair rather long. Now, if my wife is honest, or concerned enough to explain, she could tell you that this is not due to any dark, unnatural instincts I possess, but because (a) I can usually think of better things than a haircut to spend two bob on, and (b) I prefer long hair. But that obvious, innocent explanation didn't appeal to Mummy at all. So she hires detectives to watch me, to see if she can't somehow get me into the *News of the World*. All so that I shan't carry off her daughter on that poor old charger of mine, all tricked out and caparisoned in discredited passions and ideals! The old grey mare that actually once led the charge against the old order – well, she certainly ain't what she used to be. It was all she could do to carry me, but your weight (*to Alison*) was too much for her. She just dropped dead on the way.

Cliff (*quietly*) Don't let's brawl, boyo. It won't do any good.

Jimmy Why *don't* we brawl? It's the only thing left I'm any good at.

Cliff Jimmy, boy –

Jimmy (*to Alison*) You've let this genuflecting sin jobber win you over, haven't you? She's got you back, hasn't she?

Helena Oh for heaven's sake, don't be such a bully! You've no right to talk about her mother like that!

Jimmy (*capable of anything now*) I've got every right. That old bitch should be dead! (*to Alison*) Well? Aren't I right?

Cliff and Helena look at Alison tensely, but she just gazes at her plate.

I said she's an old bitch, and should be dead! What's the matter with you? Why don't you leap to her defence!

Cliff gets up quickly, and takes his arm.

Cliff Jimmy, don't!

Jimmy pushes him back savagely, and he sits down helplessly, turning his head away on to his hand.

Jimmy If someone said something like that about me, she'd react soon enough – she'd spring into her well known lethargy, and say nothing! I say she ought to be dead. (*He brakes for a fresh spurt later. He's saving his strength for the knock-out.*) My God, those worms will need a good dose of salts the day they get through her! Oh what a bellyache you've got coming to you, my little wormy ones! Alison's mother is on the way! (*in what he intends to be a comic declamatory voice*) She will pass away, my friends, leaving a trail of worms gasping for laxatives behind her – from purgatives to purgatory.

He smiles down at Alison, but still she hasn't broken. Cliff won't look at them. Only Helena looks at him. Denied the other two, he addresses her.

Helena I feel rather sick, that's all. Sick with contempt and loathing.

He can feel her struggling on the end of his line, and he looks at her rather absently.

Jimmy One day, when I'm no longer spending my days running a sweet-stall, I may write a book about us all. It's all here. (*slapping his forehead*) Written in flames a mile high. And it won't be recollected in tranquillity either, picking daffodils with Auntie Wordsworth. It'll be recollected in fire, and blood. My blood.

Helena (*thinking patient reasonableness may be worth a try*) She simply said that she's going to church with me. I don't see why that calls for this incredible outburst.

Jimmy Don't you? Perhaps you're not as clever as I thought.

Helena You think the world's treated you pretty badly, don't you?

Alison (*turning her face away L*) Oh, don't try and take his suffering away from him – he'd be lost without it.

He looks at her in surprise, but he turns back to Helena. Alison can have her turn again later.

Jimmy I thought this play you're touring in finished up on Saturday week?

54

Helena That's right.

Jimmy Eight days ago, in fact.

Helena Alison wanted me to stay.

Jimmy What are you plotting?

Helena Don't you think we've had enough of the heavy villain?

Jimmy (*to Alison*) You don't believe in all that stuff. Why you don't believe in anything. You're just doing it to be vindictive, aren't you? Why – why are you letting her influence you like this?

Alison (*starting to break*) Why, why, why, why! (*putting her hands over her ears*) That word's pulling my head off!

Jimmy And as long as you're around, I'll go on using it.

He crosses down to the armchair, and seats himself on the back of it. He addresses Helena's back.

The last time she was in church was when she was married to me. I expect that surprises you, doesn't it? It was expediency, pure and simple. We were in a hurry, you see. (*The comedy of this strikes him at once, and he laughs.*) Yes, we were actually in a hurry! Lusting for the slaughter! Well, the local registrar was a particular pal of Daddy's, and we knew he'd spill the beans to the Colonel like a shot. So we had to seek out some local vicar who didn't know him quite so well. But it was no use. When my best man – a chap I'd met in the pub that morning – and I turned up, Mummy and Daddy were in the church already. They'd found out at the last moment, and had come to watch the execution carried out. How I remember looking down at them, full of beer for breakfast, and feeling a bit buzzed. Mummy was slumped over her pew in a heap – the noble, female rhino, pole-axed at last! And Daddy sat beside her, upright and unafraid, dreaming of his days among the Indian Princes, and unable to believe he'd left his horsewhip at home. Just the two of them in that empty church – them and me. (*coming out of his remembrance suddenly*) I'm not sure what happened after that. We must have been married, I suppose. I think I remember being sick in the vestry. (*to Alison*) Was I?

Helena Haven't you finished?

He can smell blood again, and he goes on calmly, cheerfully.

Jimmy (*to Alison*) Are you going to let yourself be taken in by this saint in Dior's clothing? I will tell you the simple truth about her. (*articulating with care*) She is a cow. I wouldn't mind that so much, but she seems to have become a sacred cow as well!

Cliff You've gone too far, Jimmy. Now dry up!

Helena Oh, let him go on.

Jimmy (*to Cliff*) I suppose you're going over to that side as well. Well, why don't you? Helena will help to make it pay off for you. She's an expert in the New Economics – the Economics of the Supernatural. It's all a simple matter of payments and penalties. (*rises*) She's one of those apocalyptic share pushers who are spreading all those rumours about a transfer of power. (*His imagination is racing, and the words pour out.*) Reason and Progress, the old firm, is selling out! Everyone get out while the going's good. Those forgotten shares you had in the old traditions, the old beliefs are going up – up and up and up. (*moves up L*) There's going to be a change over. A new Board of Directors, who are going to see that the dividends are always attractive, and that they go to the right people. (*facing them*) Sell out everything you've got: all those stocks in the old, free inquiry. (*crosses to above table*) The Big Crash is coming, you can't escape it, so get in on the ground floor with Helena and her friends while there's still time. And there isn't much of it left. Tell me, what could be more gilt-edged than the next world! It's a capital gain, and it's all yours. (*He moves round the table, back to his chair R.*) You see, I know Helena and her kind so very well. In fact, her kind are everywhere, you can't move for them. They're a romantic lot. They spend their time mostly looking forward to the past. The only place they can see the light is the Dark Ages. She's moved long ago into a lovely little cottage of the soul, cut right off from the ugly problems of the twentieth century altogether. She prefers to be cut off from all the conveniences we've fought to get for centuries. She'd rather go down to the ecstatic little shed at the bottom of the garden to relieve her sense of guilt. Our Helena is full of ecstatic wind – (*he leans across the table at her*) aren't you?

He waits for her to reply.

Helena (*quite calmly*) It's a pity you've been so far away all this time. I would probably have slapped your face.

They look into each other's eyes across the table. He moves slowly up, above Cliff, until he is beside her.

You've behaved like this ever since I first came.

Jimmy Helena, have you ever watched somebody die?

She makes a move to rise.

No, don't move away.

She remains seated, and looks up at him.

It doesn't look dignified enough for you.

Helena (*like ice*) If you come any nearer, I will slap your face.

He looks down at her, a grin smouldering round his mouth.

Jimmy I hope you won't make the mistake of thinking for one moment that I am a gentleman.

57

Helena I'm not very likely to do that.

Jimmy (*bringing his face close to hers*) I've no public school scruples about hitting girls. (*gently*) If you slap my face – by God, I'll lay you out!

Helena You probably would. You're the type.

Jimmy You bet I'm the type. I'm the type that detests physical violence. Which is why, if I find some woman trying to cash in on what she thinks is my defenceless chivalry by lashing out with her frail little fists, I lash back at her.

Helena Is that meant to be subtle, or just plain Irish?

His grin widens.

Jimmy I think you and I understand one another all right. But you haven't answered my question. I said: have you watched somebody die?

Helena No, I haven't.

Jimmy Anyone who's never watched somebody die is suffering from a pretty bad case of virginity. (*His good humour of a moment ago deserts him, as he begins to remember.*) For twelve months, I watched my father dying – when I was ten years old. He'd come back from the war in Spain, you see. And certain God-fearing gentlemen there had made such a mess of him, he didn't have long left to live. Everyone knew it – even I knew it. (*He moves R.*) But, you see, I was the only one who cared. (*He turns to the window.*) His family were embarrassed by the whole business. Embarrassed and irritated. (*looking out*) As for my mother, all she could think about was the fact that she had allied herself to a man who seemed to be on the wrong side of all things. My mother was all for being associated with minorities, provided they were the smart, fashionable ones. (*He moves up C again.*) We all of us waited for him to die. The family sent him a cheque every month, and hoped he'd get on with it quietly, without too much vulgar fuss. My mother looked after him without complaining, and that was about all. Perhaps she pitied him. I suppose she was capable of that. (*with a kind of appeal in his voice*) But *I* was the only one who cared! (*He moves L, behind the armchair.*) Every time I sat on the edge of his bed, to listen to him talking or reading to me, I had to fight back my tears. At the end of twelve months, I was a veteran. (*He leans forward on the back of the armchair.*) All that that feverish failure of a man had to listen to him was a small, frightened boy. I spent hour upon hour in that tiny bedroom. He would talk to me for hours, pouring out all that was left of his life to one, lonely, bewildered little boy, who could barely understand half of what he said. All he could feel was the despair and the bitterness, the sweet, sickly smell of a dying man. (*He moves around the chair.*) You see, I learnt at an early age what it was to be angry – angry and helpless. And I can never forget it. (*He sits.*) I knew more about – love . . . betrayal . . . and death, when I was ten years old than you will probably ever know all your life.

They all sit silently. Presently, Helena rises.

Helena Time we went.

Alison nods.

I'll just get my things together. (*crosses to door*) I'll see you downstairs. (*She exits.*)

A slight pause.

Jimmy (*not looking at her, almost whispering*) Doesn't it matter to you – what people do to me? What are you trying to do to me? I've given you just everything. Doesn't it mean *anything* to you?

Her back stiffens. His axe-swinging bravado has vanished, and his voice crumples in disabled rage.

59

You Judas! You phlegm! She's taking you with her, and you're so bloody feeble, you'll let her do it!

Alison suddenly takes hold of her cup, and hurls it on the floor. He's drawn blood at last. She looks down at the pieces on the floor, and then at him. Then she crosses R, takes out a dress on a hanger, and slips it on. As she is zipping up the side, she feels giddy, and she has to lean against the wardrobe for support. She closes her eyes.

Alison (*softly*) All I want is a little peace.

Jimmy Peace! God! She wants peace! (*Hardly able to get his words out.*) My heart is so full, I feel ill – and she wants peace!

She crosses to the bed to put on her shoes. Cliff gets up from the table, and sits in the armchair R. He picks up a paper, and looks at that. Jimmy has recovered slightly, and manages to sound almost detached.

I rage, and shout my head off, and everyone thinks 'poor chap!' or 'what an objectionable young man!' But that girl there can twist your arm off with her silence. I've sat in this chair in the dark for hours. And, although she knows I'm feeling as I feel now, she's turned over, and gone to sleep.

He gets up and faces Cliff, who doesn't look up from his paper.

One of us is crazy. One of us is mean and stupid and crazy. Which is it? Is it me? Is it me, standing here like an hysterical girl, hardly able to get my words out? Or is it her? Sitting there, putting on her shoes to go out with that – (*But inspiration has deserted him by now.*) Which is it?

Cliff is still looking down at his paper.

I wish to heaven you'd try loving her, that's all.

He moves up C, watching her look for her gloves.

Perhaps, one day, you may want to come back. I shall wait for that day. I want to stand up in your tears, and splash about in them, and sing. I want to be there when you grovel. I want to be there, I want to watch it, I want the front seat.

Helena enters, carrying two prayer books.

I want to see your face rubbed in the mud – that's all I can hope for. There's nothing else I want any longer.

Helena (*after a moment*) There's a 'phone call for you.

Jimmy (*turning*) Well, it can't be anything good, can it?

He goes out.

Helena All ready?

Alison Yes – I think so.

Helena You feel all right, don't you? (*She nods.*) What's he been raving about now? Oh, what does it matter? He makes me want to claw his hair out by the roots. When I think of what you will be going through in a few months' time – and all for him! It's as if you'd done *him* wrong! These *men*! (*turning on Cliff*) And all the time you just sit there, and do nothing!

Cliff (*looking up slowly*) That's right – I just sit here.

Helena What's the matter with you? What sort of a man are you?

Cliff I'm not the District Commissioner, you know. Listen, Helena – I don't feel like Jimmy does about you, but I'm not exactly on your side either. And since you've been here, everything's certainly been worse than it's ever been. This has always been a battlefield, but I'm pretty certain that if I hadn't been here, everything would have been over between these two long ago. I've been a – a no-man's land between them. Sometimes, it's been still and peaceful, no incidents,

61

and we've all been reasonably happy. But most of the time, it's simply a very narrow strip of plain hell. But where I come from, we're used to brawling and excitement. Perhaps I even enjoy being in the thick of it. I love these two people very much. (*He looks at her steadily, and adds simply*) And I pity all of us.

Helena Are you including me in that? (*But she goes on quickly to avoid his reply.*) I don't understand him, you or any of it. All I know is that none of you seems to know how to behave in a decent, civilized way. (*in command now*) Listen, Alison – I've sent your father a wire.

Alison (*numbed and vague by now*) Oh?

Helena looks at her, and realizes quickly that everything now will have to depend on her own authority. She tries to explain patiently.

Helena Look, dear – he'll get it first thing in the morning. I thought it would be better than trying to explain the situation over the 'phone. I asked him to come up, and fetch you home tomorrow.

Alison What did you say?

Helena Simply that you wanted to come home, and would he come up for you.

Alison I see.

Helena I knew that would be quite enough. I told him there was nothing to worry about, so they won't worry and think there's been an accident or anything. I had to do something, dear. (*very gently*) You didn't mind, did you?

Alison No, I don't mind. Thank you.

Helena And you will go when he comes for you?

Alison (*pause*) Yes, I'll go.

Helena (*relieved*) I expect he'll drive up. He should be here about tea-time. It'll give you plenty of time to get your things together. And, perhaps, after you've gone – Jimmy (*saying the word almost with difficulty*) will come to his senses, and face up to things.

Alison Who was on the 'phone?

Helena I didn't catch it properly. It rang after I'd sent the wire off – just as soon as I put the receiver down almost. I had to go back down the stairs again. Sister somebody, I think.

Alison Must have been a hospital or something. Unless he knows someone in a convent – *that* doesn't seem very likely, does it? Well, we'll be late, if we don't hurry.

She puts down one of the prayer books on the table. Enter Jimmy. He comes down C, between the two women.

Cliff All right, boyo?

Jimmy (*to Alison*) It's Hugh's mum. She's – had a stroke.

Slight pause.

Alison I'm sorry.

Jimmy sits on the bed.

Cliff How bad is it?

Jimmy They didn't say much. But I think she's dying.

Cliff Oh dear . . .

Jimmy (*rubbing his fist over his face*) It doesn't make any sense at all. Do you think it does?

Alison I'm sorry – I really am.

Cliff Anything I can do?

Jimmy The London train goes in half an hour. You'd better order me a taxi.

Cliff Right. (*He crosses to the door, and stops.*) Do you want me to come with you, boy?

Jimmy No thanks. After all, you hardly knew her. It's not for you to go.

Helena looks quickly at Alison.

She may not even remember me, for all I know.

Cliff OK. (*He exits.*)

Jimmy I remember the first time I showed her your photograph – just after we were married. She looked at it, and the tears just welled up in her eyes, and she said: 'But she's so beautiful! She's so beautiful!' She kept repeating it as if she couldn't believe it. Sounds a bit simple and sentimental when you repeat it. But it was pure gold the way she said it.

He looks at her. She is standing by the dressing table, her back to him.

She got a kick out of you, like she did out of everything else. Hand me my shoes, will you?

She kneels down, and hands them to him.

(*looking down at his feet*) You're coming with me, aren't you? She (*he shrugs*) hasn't got anyone else now. I need you . . . to come with me.

He looks into her eyes, but she turns away, and stands up. Outside, the church bells start ringing. Helena moves up to the door, and waits watching them closely. Alison stands quite still, Jimmy's eyes burning into her. Then, she crosses in front of him to the table where she picks up the prayer book, her back to him. She wavers, and seems about to say something, but turns upstage instead, and walks quietly to the door.

Alison (*hardly audible*) Let's go.

She goes out, Helena following. Jimmy gets up, looks about him unbelievingly, and leans against the chest of drawers. The teddy bear is close to his face, and he picks it up gently, looks at it quickly, and throws it downstage. It hits the floor with a thud, and it makes a rattling, groaning sound – as guaranteed in the advertisement. Jimmy falls forward on to the bed, his face buried in the covers.

Quick Curtain

SCENE TWO

The following evening. When the curtain rises, Alison is discovered R, going from her dressing table to the bed, and packing her things into a suitcase. Sitting down L is her father, **Colonel Redfern,** *a large handsome man, about sixty. Forty years of being a soldier sometimes conceals the essentially gentle, kindly man underneath. Brought up to command respect, he is often slightly withdrawn and uneasy now that he finds himself in a world where his authority has lately become less and less unquestionable. His wife would relish the present situation, but he is only disturbed and bewildered by it. He looks around him, discreetly scrutinizing everything.*

Colonel (*partly to himself*) I'm afraid it's all beyond me. I suppose it always will be. As for Jimmy – he just speaks a different language from any of us. Where did you say he'd gone?

Alison He's gone to see Mrs Tanner.

Colonel Who?

Alison Hugh Tanner's mother.

Colonel Oh, I see.

65

Alison She's been taken ill – a stroke. Hugh's abroad, as you know, so Jimmy's gone to London to see her.

He nods.

He wanted me to go with him.

Colonel Didn't she start him off in this sweet-stall business?

Alison Yes.

Colonel What is she like? Nothing like her son, I trust?

Alison Not remotely. Oh – how can you describe her? Rather – ordinary. What Jimmy insists on calling working class. A Charwoman who married an actor, worked hard all her life, and spent most of it struggling to support her husband and her son. Jimmy and she are very fond of each other.

Colonel So you didn't go with him?

Alison No.

Colonel Who's looking after the sweet-stall?

Alison Cliff. He should be in soon.

Colonel Oh yes, of course – Cliff. Does he live here too?

Alison Yes. His room is just across the landing.

Colonel Sweet-stall. It does seem an extraordinary thing for an educated young man to be occupying himself with. Why should he want to do that, of all things. I've always thought he must be quite clever in his way.

Alison (*no longer interested in this problem*) Oh, he tried so many things – journalism, advertising, even vacuum cleaners for a few weeks. He seems to have been as happy doing this as anything else.

Colonel I've often wondered what it was like – where you were living, I mean. You didn't tell us very much in your letters.

Alison There wasn't a great deal to tell you. There's not much social life here.

Colonel Oh, I know what you mean. You were afraid of being disloyal to your husband.

Alison Disloyal! (*She laughs.*) He thought it was high treason of me to write to you at all! I used to have to dodge downstairs for the post, so that he wouldn't see I was getting letters from home. Even then I had to hide them.

Colonel He really does hate us doesn't he?

Alison Oh yes – don't have any doubts about that. He hates all of us.

Colonel (*sighs*) It seems a great pity. It was all so unfortunate – unfortunate and unnecessary. I'm afraid I can't help feeling that he must have had a certain amount of right on his side.

Alison (*puzzled by this admission*) Right on his side?

Colonel It's a little late to admit it, I know, but your mother and I weren't entirely free from blame. I have never said anything – there was no point afterwards – but I have always believed that she went too far over Jimmy. Of course, she was extremely upset at the time – we both were – and that explains a good deal of what happened. I did my best to stop her, but she was in such a state of mind, there was simply nothing I could so. She seemed to have made up her mind that if he was going to marry you, he must be a criminal, at the very least. All those inquiries, the private detectives – the accusations. I hated every moment of it.

Alison I suppose she was trying to protect me – in a rather heavy-handed way, admittedly.

Colonel I must confess I find that kind of thing rather horrifying. Anyway, I try to think now that it never happened. I didn't approve of Jimmy at all, and I don't suppose I ever should, but, looking back on it, I think it would have been better, for all concerned, if we had never attempted to interfere. At least, it would have been a little more dignified.

Alison It wasn't your fault.

Colonel I don't know. We were all to blame, in our different ways. No doubt Jimmy acted in good faith. He's honest enough, whatever else he may be. And your mother – in her heavy-handed way, as you put it – acted in good faith as well. Perhaps you and I were the ones most to blame.

Alison You and I!

Colonel I think you may take after me a little, my dear. You like to sit on the fence because it's comfortable and more peaceful.

Alison Sitting on the fence! I married him, didn't I.

Colonel Oh yes, you did.

Alison In spite of all the humiliating scenes and the threats! What did you say to me at the time? Wasn't I letting you down, turning against you, how could I do this to you etcetera?

Colonel Perhaps it might have been better if you hadn't written letters to us – knowing how we felt about your husband, and after everything that had happened. (*He looks at her uncomfortably.*) Forgive me, I'm a little confused, what with everything – the telegram, driving up here suddenly . . .

He trails off rather helplessly. He looks tired. He glances at her nervously, a hint of accusation in his eyes, as if he expected her to defend herself further. She senses this, and is more confused than ever.

Alison Do you know what he said about Mummy? He said she was an overfed, overprivileged old bitch. 'A good blow-out for the worms' was his expression, I think.

68

Colonel I see. And what does he say about me?

Alison Oh, he doesn't seem to mind you so much. In fact, I think he rather likes you. He likes you because he can feel sorry for you. (*conscious that what she says is going to hurt him*) 'Poor old Daddy – just one of those sturdy old plants left over from the Edwardian Wilderness that can't understand why the sun isn't shining any more.' (*rather lamely*) Something like that, anyway.

Colonel He has quite a turn of phrase, hasn't he? (*simply, and without malice*) Why did you ever have to meet this young man?

Alison Oh, Daddy, please don't put me on trial now. I've been on trial every day and night of my life for nearly four years.

Colonel But why should he have married you, feeling as he did about everything?

Alison That is the famous American question – you know, the sixty-four dollar one! Perhaps it was revenge.

He looks up uncomprehendingly.

Oh yes. Some people do actually marry for revenge. People like Jimmy, anyway. Or perhaps he should have been another Shelley, and can't understand now why I'm not another Mary, and you're not William Godwin. He thinks he's got a sort of genius for love and friendship – on his own terms. Well, for twenty years, I'd lived a happy, uncomplicated life, and suddenly, this – this spiritual barbarian – throws down the gauntlet at me. Perhaps only another woman could understand what a challenge like that means – although I think Helena was as mystified as you are.

Colonel I am mystified. (*He rises, and crosses to the window R.*) Your husband has obviously taught you a great deal, whether you realize it or not. What any of it means, I don't know. I always believed that people married each other because they were in love. That always seemed a good enough reason to me. But apparently, that's too simple for young people nowadays. They have to talk about challenges and revenge. I just can't believe that love between men and women is really like that.

Alison Only some men and women.

Colonel But why you? My daughter . . . No. Perhaps Jimmy is right. Perhaps I am a – what was it? an old plant left over from the Edwardian Wilderness. And I can't understand why the sun isn't shining any more. You can see what he means, can't you? It was March, 1914, when I left England, and, apart from leaves every ten years or so, I didn't see much of my own country until we all came back in '47. Oh, I knew things had changed, of course. People told you all the time the way it was going – going to the dogs, as the Blimps are supposed to say. But it seemed very unreal to me, out there. The England I remembered was the one I left in 1914, and I was happy to go on remembering it that way. Beside, I had the Maharajah's army to command – that was my world, and I loved it, all of it. At the time, it looked like going on for ever. When I think of it now, it seems like a dream. If only it could have gone on for ever. Those long, cool evenings up in the hills, everything purple and golden. Your mother and I were so happy then. It seemed as though we had everything we could ever want. I think the last day the sun shone was when that dirty little train steamed out of that crowded, suffocating Indian station, and the battalion band playing for all it was worth. I knew in my heart it was all over then. Everything.

Alison You're hurt because everything is changed. Jimmy is hurt because everything is the same. And neither of you can face it. Something's gone wrong somewhere, hasn't it?

Colonel It looks like it, my dear.

She picks up the squirrel from the chest of drawers, is

about to put it in her suitcase, hesitates, and then puts it back. The Colonel turns and looks at her. She moves down towards him, her head turned away. For a few moments, she seems to be standing on the edge of choice. The choice made, her body wheels round suddenly, and she is leaning against him, weeping softly.

(*presently*) This is a big step you're taking. You've made up your mind to come back with me? Is that really what you want?

Enter Helena.

Helena I'm sorry. I came in to see if I could help you pack, Alison. Oh, you look as though you've finished.

Alison leaves her father, and moves to the bed, pushing down the lid of her suitcase.

Alison All ready.

Helena Have you got everything?

Alison Well, no. But Cliff can send the rest on sometime, I expect. He should have been back by now. Oh, of course, he's had to put the stall away on his own today.

Colonel (*crossing and picking up the suitcase*) Well, I'd better put this in the car then. We may as well get along. Your mother will be worried, I know. I promised her I'd ring her when I got here. She's not very well.

Helena I hope my telegram didn't upset her too much. Perhaps I shouldn't have –

Colonel Not at all. We were very grateful that you did. It was very kind of you, indeed. She tried to insist on coming with me, but I finally managed to talk her out of it. I thought it would be best for everyone. What about your case, Helena? If you care to tell me where it is, I'll take it down with this one.

Helena I'm afraid I shan't be coming tonight.

Alison (*very surprised*) Aren't you coming with us?

Enter Cliff.

Helena I'd like to, but the fact is I've an appointment tomorrow in Birmingham – about a job. They've just sent me a script. It's rather important, and I don't want to miss it. So it looks as though I shall have to stay here tonight.

Alison Oh, I see. Hullo, Cliff.

Cliff Hullo there.

Alison Daddy – this is Cliff.

Colonel How do you do, Cliff.

Cliff How do you do, sir.

Slight pause.

Colonel Well, I'd better put this in the car, hadn't I? Don't be long, Alison. Goodbye, Helena. I expect we shall be seeing you again soon, if you're not busy.

Helena Oh, yes, I shall be back in a day or two.

Cliff takes off his jacket.

Colonel Well, then – goodbye, Cliff.

Cliff Goodbye, sir.

The Colonel goes out. Cliff comes down L. Helena moves C.

You're really going then?

Alison Really going.

Cliff I should think Jimmy would be back pretty soon. You won't wait?

Alison No, Cliff.

Cliff Who's going to tell him?

Helena I can tell him. That is, if I'm here when he comes back.

Cliff (*quietly*) You'll be here. (*to Alison*) Don't you think you ought to tell him yourself?

She hands him an envelope from her handbag. He takes it.

Bit conventional, isn't it?

Alison I'm a conventional girl.

He crosses to her, and puts his arms round her.

Cliff (*back over his shoulder, to Helena*) I hope you're right, that's all.

Helena What do you mean? You hope *I'm* right?

Cliff (*to Alison*) The place is going to be really cock-eyed now. You know that, don't you?

Alison Please, Cliff –

He nods. She kisses him.

I'll write to you later.

Cliff Goodbye, lovely.

Alison Look after him.

Cliff We'll keep the old nut-house going somehow.

She crosses C, in between the two of them, glances quickly at the two armchairs, the papers still left around them from yesterday. Helena kisses her on the cheek, and squeezes her hand.

Helena See you soon.

Alison nods, and goes out quickly. Cliff and Helena are left looking at each other.

Would you like me to make you some tea?

Cliff No, thanks.

Helena Think I might have some myself, if you don't mind.

Cliff So you're staying.

Helena Just for tonight. Do you object?

Cliff Nothing to do with me. (*against the table C*) Of course, he may not be back until later on.

She crosses L, to the window, and lights a cigarette.

Helena What do you think he'll do? Perhaps he'll look out one of his old girl friends. What about this Madeline?

Cliff What about her?

Helena Isn't she supposed to have done a lot for him? Couldn't he go back to her?

Cliff I shouldn't think so.

Helena What happened?

Cliff She was nearly old enough to be his mother. I expect that's something to do with it! Why the hell should I know!

For the first time in the play, his good humour has completely deserted him. She looks surprised.

Helena You're his friend, aren't you? Anyway, he's not what you'd call reticent about himself, is he? I've never seen so many souls stripped to the waist since I've been here.

He turns to go.

Aren't you staying?

Cliff No, I'm not. There was a train in from London about

74

five minutes ago. And, just in case he may have been on it, I'm going out.

Helena Don't you think you ought to be here when he comes?

Cliff I've had a hard day, and I don't think I want to see anyone hurt until I've had something to eat first, and perhaps a few drinks as well. I think I might pick up some nice, pleasant little tart in a milk bar, and sneak her in past old mother Drury. Here! (*tossing the letter at her*) You give it to him! (*crossing to door*) He's all yours. (*at door*) And I hope he rams it up your nostrils! (*He exits.*)

She crosses to the table, and stubs out her cigarette. The front door downstairs is heard to slam. She moves to the wardrobe, opens it idly. It is empty, except for one dress, swinging on a hanger. She goes over to the dressing table, now cleared but for a framed photograph of Jimmy. Idly, she slams the empty drawers open and shut. She turns upstage to the chest of drawers, picks up the toy bear, and sits on the bed, looking at it. She lays her head back on the pillow, still holding the bear. She looks up quickly as the door crashes open, and Jimmy enters. He stands looking at her, then moves down C, taking off his raincoat and throwing it over the table. He is almost giddy with anger, and has to steady himself on the chair. He looks up.

Jimmy That old bastard nearly ran me down in his car! Now, if he'd killed me, that really would have been ironical. And how right and fitting that my wife should have been a passenger. A passenger! What's the matter with everybody? (*crossing up to her*) Cliff practically walked into me, coming out of the house. He belted up the other way, and pretended not to see me. Are you the only one who's not afraid to stay?

She hands him Alison's note. He takes it.

Oh, it's one of these, is it? (*He rips it open. He reads a few*

75

lines, and almost snorts with disbelief.) Did you write this for her! Well, listen to this then! (*reading*) 'My dear – I must get away. I don't suppose you will understand, but please try. I need peace so desperately, and, at the moment, I am willing to sacrifice everything just for that. I don't know what's going to happen to us. I know you will be feeling wretched and bitter, but try to be a little patient with me. I shall always have a deep, loving need of you – Alison.' Oh, how could she be so bloody wet! Deep loving need! That makes me puke! (*crossing to R*) She couldn't say 'You rotten bastard! I hate your guts, I'm clearing out, and I hope you rot!' No, she had to make a polite, emotional mess out of it! (*Seeing the dress in the wardrobe, he rips it out, and throws it in the corner up L.*) Deep, loving need! I never thought she was capable of being as phoney as that! What is that – a line from one of those plays you've been in? What are you doing here anyway? You'd better keep out of my way, if you don't want your head kicked in.

Helena (*calmly*) If you'll stop thinking about yourself for one moment, I'll tell you something I think you ought to know. Your wife is going to have a baby.

He just looks at her.

Well? Doesn't that mean anything? Even to you?

He is taken aback, but not so much by the news, as by her.

Jimmy All right – yes. I am surprised. I give you that. But, tell me. Did you honestly expect me to go soggy at the knees, and collapse with remorse! (*leaning nearer*) Listen, if you'll stop breathing your female wisdom all over me, I'll tell you something: I don't care. (*beginning quietly*) I don't care if she's going to have a baby. I don't care if it has two heads! (*He knows her fingers are itching*) Do I disgust you? Well, go on – slap my face. But remember what I told you before, will you? For eleven hours, I have been watching someone I love

76

very much going through the sordid process of dying. She was alone, and I was the only one with her. And when I have to walk behind that coffin on Thursday, I'll be on my own again. Because that bitch won't even send her a bunch of flowers – I know! She made the great mistake of all her kind. She thought that because Hugh's mother was a deprived and ignorant old woman, who said all the wrong things in all the wrong places, she couldn't be taken seriously. And you think I should be overcome with awe because that cruel, stupid girl is going to have a baby! (*anguish in his voice*) I can't believe it! I can't. (*grabbing her shoulder*) Well, the performance is over. Now leave me alone, and *get out*, you evil-minded little virgin.

She slaps his face savagely. An expression of horror and disbelief floods his face. But it drains away, and all that is left is pain. His hand goes up to his head, and a muffled cry of despair escapes him. Helena tears his hand away, and kisses him passionately, drawing him down beside her.

Act III
SCENE ONE

Several months later. A Sunday evening. Alison's personal belongings, such as her make-up things on the dressing table, for example, have been replaced by Helena's.

At rise of curtain, we find Jimmy and Cliff sprawled in their respective armchairs, immersed in the Sunday newspapers. Helena is standing down L leaning over the ironing board, a small pile of clothes beside her. She looks more attractive than before, for the setting of her face is more relaxed. She still looks quite smart, but in an unpremeditated, careless way; she wears an old shirt of Jimmy's.

Cliff That stinking old pipe!

Pause.

Jimmy Shut up.

Cliff Why don't you do something with it?

Jimmy Why do I spend half of Sunday reading the papers?

Cliff (*kicks him without lowering his paper*) It stinks!

Jimmy So do you, but I'm not singing an aria about it. (*turns to the next page*) The dirty ones get more and more wet round the mouth, and the posh ones are more pompous than ever. (*lowering paper, and waving pipe at Helena*) Does this bother you?

Helena No. I quite like it.

Jimmy (*to Cliff*) There you are – she likes it!

He returns to his paper. Cliff grunts.

Have you read about the grotesque and evil practices going on in the Midlands?

Cliff Read about the what?

Jimmy Grotesque and evil practices going on in the Midlands.

Cliff No, what about 'em?

Jimmy Seems we don't know the old place. It's all in here. Startling Revelations this week! Pictures too. Reconstructions of midnight invocations to the Coptic Goddess of fertility.

Helena Sounds madly depraved.

Jimmy Yes, it's rather us, isn't it? My gosh, look at 'em! Snarling themselves silly. Next week a well-known debutante relates how, during an evil orgy in Market Harborough, she killed and drank the blood of a white cockerel. Well – I'll bet Fortnums must be doing a roaring line in sacrificial cocks! (*thoughtful*) Perhaps that's what Miss Drury does on Sunday evenings. She puts in a stint as evil high priestess down at the YW – probably having a workout at this very moment. (*to Helena*) You never dabbled in this kind of thing, did you?

Helena (*laughs*) Not lately!

Jimmy Sounds rather your cup of tea – cup of blood, I should say. (*in an imitation of a Midlands accent*) Well, I mean, it gives you something to do, doesn't it? After all, it wouldn't do if we was all alike, would it? It'd be a funny world if we was all the same, that's what *I* always say! (*resuming in his normal voice*) All I know is that somebody's been sticking pins into *my* wax image for years. (*suddenly*) Of course: Alison's mother! Every Friday, the wax arrives from Harrods, and all through the week-end, she's stabbing away at it with a hatpin! Ruined her bridge game, I dare say.

Helena Why don't *you* try it?

Jimmy Yes, it's an idea. (*pointing to Cliff*) Just for a start, we could roast him over the gas stove. Have we got enough shillings for the meter? It seems to be just the thing for these autumn evenings. After all the whole point of a sacrifice is that you give up something you never really wanted in the first place. You know what I mean? People are doing it around you all the time. They give up their careers, say – or their beliefs – or sex. And everyone thinks to themselves: how wonderful to be able to do that. If only I were capable of doing that! But the truth of it is that they've been kidding themselves, and they've been kidding you. It's not awfully difficult – giving up something you were incapable of ever really wanting. We shouldn't be admiring them. We should feel rather sorry for them. (*Coming back from this sudden, brooding excursion, he turns to Cliff.*) You'll make an admirable sacrifice.

Cliff (*mumbling*) Dry up! I'm trying to read.

Jimmy Afterwards, we can make a loving cup from his blood. Can't say I fancy that so much. I've seen it – it looks like cochineal, ever so common. (*to Helena*) Yours would be much better – pale Cambridge blue, I imagine. No? And afterwards, we could make invocations to the Coptic Goddess of fertility. Got any idea how you do that? (*to Cliff*) Do you know?

Cliff Shouldn't have thought *you* needed to make invocations to the Coptic whatever-she-is!

Jimmy Yes, I see what you mean. (*to Helena*) Well, we don't want to *ask* for trouble, do we? Perhaps it might appeal to the lady here – she's written a long letter all about artificial insemination. It's headed: Haven't we tried God's patience enough! (*He throws the paper down.*) Let's see the other posh one.

Cliff Haven't finished yet.

Jimmy Well, hurry up. I'll have to write and ask them to put hyphens in between the syllables for you. There's a particularly savage correspondence going on in there about whether Milton wore braces or not. I just want to see who gets shot down this week.

Cliff Just read that. Don't know what it was about, but a Fellow of All Souls seems to have bitten the dust, and the Athenaeum's going up in flames, so the Editor declares that this correspondence is now closed.

Jimmy I think you're actually acquiring yourself a curiosity, my boy. Oh yes, and then there's an American professor from Yale or somewhere, who believes that when Shakespeare was writing *The Tempest*, he changed his sex. Yes, he was obliged to go back to Stratford because the other actors couldn't take him seriously any longer. This professor chap is coming over here to search for certain documents which will prove that poor old WS ended up in someone else's second best bed – a certain Warwickshire farmer's, whom he married after having three children by him.

Helena laughs. Jimmy looks up quizzically.

Is anything the matter?

Helena No, nothing. I'm only beginning to get used to him. I never (*this is to Cliff*) used to be sure when he was being serious, or when he wasn't.

Cliff Don't think he knows himself half the time. When in doubt, just mark it down as an insult.

Jimmy Hurry up with that paper, and shut up! What are we going to do tonight? There isn't even a decent concert on. (*to Helena*) Are you going to Church?

Helena (*rather taken aback*) No. I don't think so. Unless you want to.

Jimmy Do I detect a growing, satanic glint in her eyes lately? Do you think it's living in sin with me that does it? (*to Helena*)

Do you feel very sinful my dear? Well? Do you?

She can hardly believe that this is an attack, and she can only look at him, uncertain of herself.

Do you feel sin crawling out of your ears, like stored up wax or something? Are you wondering whether I'm joking or not? Perhaps I ought to wear a red nose and funny hat. I'm just curious, that's all.

She is shaken by the sudden coldness in his eyes, but before she has time to fully realize how hurt she is, he is smiling at her, and shouting cheerfully at Cliff.

Let's have that paper, stupid!

Cliff Why don't you drop dead!

Jimmy (*to Helena*) Will you be much longer doing that?

Helena Nearly finished.

Jimmy Talking of sin, wasn't that Miss Drury's Reverend friend I saw you chatting with yesterday. Helena darling, I said wasn't that . . .

Helena Yes it was.

Jimmy My dear, you don't have to be on the defensive you know.

Helena I'm not on the defensive.

Jimmy After all, there's no reason why we shouldn't have the parson to tea up here. Why don't we? Did you find that you had much in common?

Helena No I don't think so.

Jimmy Do you think that some of this spiritual beefcake would make a man of me? Should I go in for this moral weight lifting and get myself some over-developed muscle? I was a liberal skinny weakling. I too was afraid to strip down

82

to my soul, but now everyone looks at my superb physique in envy. I can perform any kind of press there is without betraying the least sign of passion or kindliness.

Helena All right Jimmy.

Jimmy Two years ago I couldn't even lift up my head – now I have more uplift than a film starlet.

Helena Jimmy, can we have one day, just one day, without tumbling over religion or politics?

Cliff Yes, change the record old boy, or pipe down.

Jimmy (*rising*) Thought of the title for a new song today. It's called 'My mother's in the madhouse – that's why I'm in love with you'. The lyrics are catchy too. I was thinking we might work it into the act.

Helena Good idea.

Jimmy I was thinking we'd scrub Jock and Day, and call ourselves something else. 'And jocund day stands tiptoed on the misty mountain tops.' It's too intellectual! Anyway, I shouldn't think people will want to be reminded of that peculiar man's plays after Harvard and Yale have finished with him. How about something bright and snappy? I know – What about – T. S. Eliot and Pam!

Cliff (*casually falling in with this familiar routine*) Mirth, mellerdy and madness!

Jimmy (*sitting at the table R and 'strumming' it*). Bringing quips and strips for you!

They sing together.

'For we may be guilty, darling . . . But we're both insane as well!' (*Jimmy stands up, and rattles his lines off at almost unintelligible speed.*) Ladies and gentlemen, as I was coming to the theatre tonight, I was passing through the stage door, and a man comes up to me, and 'e says:

Cliff 'Ere! Have you seen nobody?

Jimmy Have I seen who?

Cliff Have you seen nobody?

Jimmy Of course, I haven't seen nobody! Kindly don't waste my time! Ladies and gentlemen, a little recitation entitled 'She said she was called a little Gidding, but she was more like a gelding iron!' Thank you. 'She said she was called little Gidding –'

Cliff Are you sure you haven't seen nobody?

Jimmy Are you still here?

Cliff I'm looking for nobody!

Jimmy *Will* you kindly go away! 'She said she was called little Gidding –'

Cliff Well, I can't find nobody anywhere, and I'm supposed to give him this case!

Jimmy Will you kindly stop interrupting per*lease*! Can't you see I'm trying to entertain these ladies and gentlemen? Who is this nobody you're talking about?

Cliff I was told to come here and give this case to nobody.

Jimmy You were told to come here and give this case to nobody.

Cliff That's right. And when I gave it to him, nobody would give me a shilling.

Jimmy And when you gave it to him, nobody would give you a shilling.

Cliff That's right.

Jimmy Well, what about it?

Cliff Nobody's not here!

Jimmy Now, let me get this straight: when you say nobody's here, you don't mean nobody's here?

Cliff No.

Jimmy No. You mean – nobody's here.

Cliff That's right.

Jimmy Well, why didn't you say so before?

Helena (*not quite sure if this is really her cue*) Hey! You down there!

Jimmy Oh, it goes on for hours yet, but never mind. What is it, sir?

Helena (*shouting*) I think your sketch stinks! I say – I think your sketch stinks!

Jimmy He thinks it stinks. And, who, pray, might you be?

Helena Me? Oh – (*with mock modesty*) I'm nobody.

Jimmy Then here's your bloody case!

He hurls a cushion at her, which hits the ironing board.

Helena My ironing board!

The two men do a Flanagan and Allen, moving slowly in step, as they sing.

Now there's a certain little lady, and you all know who I
mean,
She may have been to Roedean, but to me she's still a queen.
Someday I'm goin' to marry her,
When times are not so bad,
Her mother doesn't care for me
So I'll 'ave to ask 'er dad.
We'll build a little home for two,

And have some quiet menage,
We'll send our kids to public school
And live on bread and marge.
Don't be afraid to sleep with your sweetheart,
Just because she's better than you.
Those forgotten middle-classes may have fallen on their noses,
But a girl who's true blue,
Will still have something left for you,
The angels up above, will know that you're in love
So don't be afraid to sleep with your sweetheart,
Just because she's better than you . . .
          They call me Sydney,
Just because she's better than you.

But Jimmy has had enough of this gag by now, and he pushes Cliff away.

Jimmy Your damned great feet! That's the second time you've kicked my ankle! It's no good – Helena will have to do it. Go on, go and make some tea, and we'll decide what we're going to do.

Cliff Make some yourself!

He pushes him back violently, Jimmy loses his balance, and falls over.

Jimmy You rough bastard!

He leaps up, and they grapple, falling on to the floor with a crash. They roll about, grunting and gasping. Cliff manages to kneel on Jimmy's chest.

Cliff (*breathing heavily*) I want to read the papers!

Jimmy You're a savage, a hooligan! You really are! Do you know that! You don't deserve to live in the same house with decent, sensitive people!

Cliff Are you going to dry up, or do I read the papers down here?

Jimmy makes a supreme effort, and Cliff topples to the floor.

Jimmy You've made me wrench my guts!

He pushes the struggling Cliff down.

Cliff Look what you're doing! You're ripping my shirt. Get *off*!

Jimmy Well, what do you want to wear a shirt for? (*rising*) A tough character like you! Now go and make me some tea.

Cliff It's the only clean one I've got. Oh, you big oaf!

Getting up from the floor, and appealing to Helena.

Look! It's filthy!

Helena Yes, it is. He's stronger than he looks. If you like to take it off now, I'll wash it through for you. It'll be dry by the time we want to go out.

Cliff hesitates.

What's the matter, Cliff?

Cliff Oh, it'll be all right.

Jimmy Give it to her, and quit moaning!

Cliff Oh, all right.

He takes it off, and gives it to her.

Thanks, Helena.

Helena (*taking it*) Right. I won't be a minute with it.

She goes out. Jimmy flops into his armchair. R.

Jimmy (*amused*) You look like Marlon Brando or something.

(*slight pause*) You don't care for Helena, do you?

Cliff You didn't seem very keen yourself once. (*hesitating, then quickly*) It's not the same, is it?

Jimmy (*irritably*) No, of course it's not the same, you idiot! It never is! Today's meal is always different from yesterday's and the last woman isn't the same as the one before. If you can't accept that, you're going to be pretty unhappy, my boy.

Cliff (*sits on the arm of his chair, and rubs his feet*) Jimmy – I don't think I shall stay here much longer.

Jimmy (*rather casually*) Oh, why not?

Cliff (*picking up his tone*) Oh, I don't know. I've just thought of trying somewhere different. The sweet-stall's all right, but I think I'd like to try something else. You're highly educated, and it suits you, but I need something a bit better.

Jimmy Just as you like, my dear boy. It's your business, not mine.

Cliff And another thing – I think Helena finds it rather a lot of work to do with two chaps about the place. It won't be so much for her if there's just the two of you. Anyway, I think I ought to find some girl who'll just look after me.

Jimmy Sounds like a good idea. Can't think who'd be stupid enough to team themselves up with you though. Perhaps Helena can think of somebody for you – one of her posh girl friends with lots of money, and no brains. That's what you want.

Cliff Something like that.

Jimmy Any idea what you're going to do?

Cliff Not much.

Jimmy That sounds like you all right! Shouldn't think you'll last five minutes without me to explain the score to you.

Cliff (*grinning*) Don't suppose so.

Jimmy You're such a scruffy little beast – I'll bet some respectable little madam from Pinner or Guildford gobbles you up in six months. She'll marry you, send you out to work, and you'll end up as clean as a new pin.

Cliff (*chuckling*) Yes, I'm stupid enough for that too!

Jimmy (*to himself*) I seem to spend my life saying goodbye.

Slight pause.

Cliff My feet hurt.

Jimmy Try washing your socks. (*slowly*) It's a funny thing. You've been loyal, generous and a good friend. But I'm quite prepared to see you wander off, find a new home, and make out on your own. And all because of something I want from that girl downstairs, something I know in my heart she's incapable of giving. You're worth a half a dozen Helenas to me or to anyone. And, if you were in my place, you'd do the same thing. Right?

Cliff Right.

Jimmy Why, why, why, why do we let these women bleed us to death? Have you ever had a letter, and on it is franked 'Please Give Your Blood Generously'? Well, the Postmaster-General does that, on behalf of all the women of the world. I suppose people of our generation aren't able to die for good causes any longer. We had all that done for us, in the thirties and the forties, when we were still kids. (*in his familiar, semi-serious mood*) There aren't any good, brave causes left. If the big bang does come, and we all get killed off, it won't be in aid of the old-fashioned, grand design. It'll just be for the Brave New-nothing-very-much-thank-you. About as pointless and inglorious as stepping in front of a bus. No, there's nothing left for it, me boy, but to let yourself be butchered by the women.

89

Enter Helena.

Helena Here you are, Cliff. (*handing him the shirt*)

Cliff Oh, thanks, Helena, very much. That's decent of you.

Helena Not at all. I should dry it over the gas – the fire in your room would be better. There won't be much room for it over that stove.

Cliff Right, I will. (*He crosses to door.*)

Jimmy And hurry up about it, stupid. We'll all go out, and have a drink soon. (*to Helena*) OK?

Helena OK.

Jimmy (*shouting to Cliff on his way out*) But make me some tea first, you madcap little Charlie.

She crosses down L.

Darling, I'm sick of seeing you behind that damned ironing board!

Helena (*wryly*) Sorry.

Jimmy Get yourself glammed up, and we'll hit the town. See you've put a shroud over Mummy, I think you should have laid a Union Jack over it.

Helena Is anything wrong?

Jimmy Oh, don't frown like that – you look like the presiding magistrate!

Helena How should I look?

Jimmy As if your heart stirred a little when you looked at me.

Helena Oh, it does that all right.

Jimmy Cliff tells me he's leaving us.

Helena I know. He told me last night.

Jimmy Did he? I always seem to be at the end of the queue when they're passing information out.

Helena I'm sorry he's going.

Jimmy Yes, so am I. He's a sloppy, irritating bastard, but he's got a big heart. You can forgive somebody almost anything for that. He's had to learn how to take it, and he knows how to hand it out. Come here.

He is sitting on the arm of his chair. She crosses to him, and they look at each other. Then she puts out her hand, and runs it over his head, fondling his ear and neck.

Right from that first night, you have always put out your hand to me first. As if you expected nothing, or worse than nothing, and didn't care. You made a good enemy, didn't you? What they call a worthy opponent. But then, when people put down their weapons, it doesn't mean they've necessarily stopped fighting.

Helena (*steadily*) I love you.

Jimmy I think perhaps you do. Yes, I think perhaps you do. Perhaps it means something to lie with your victorious general in your arms. Especially, when he's heartily sick of the whole campaign, tired out, hungry and dry.

His lips find her fingers, and he kisses them. She presses his head against her.

You stood up, and came out to meet me. Oh, Helena –

His face comes up to hers, and they embrace fiercely.

Don't let anything go wrong!

Helena (*softly*) Oh, my darling –

Jimmy Either you're with me or against me.

Helena I've always wanted you – always!

They kiss again.

Jimmy T. S. Eliot and Pam, we'll make a good double. If you'll help me. I'll close that damned sweet-stall, and we'll start everything from scratch. What do you say? We'll get away from this place.

Helena (*nodding happily*) I say that's wonderful.

Jimmy (*kissing her quickly*) Put all that junk away, and we'll get out. We'll get pleasantly, joyfully tiddly, we'll gaze at each other tenderly and lecherously in The Builder's Arms, and then we'll come back here, and I'll make such love to you, you'll not care about anything else at all.

She moves away L, after kissing his hand.

Helena I'll just change out of your old shirt. (*folding ironing board*)

Jimmy (*moving US to door*) Right. I'll hurry up the little man.

But before he reaches the door, it opens and Alison enters. She wears a raincoat, her hair is untidy, and she looks rather ill. There is a stunned pause.

Alison (*quietly*) Hullo.

Jimmy (*to Helena, after a moment*) Friend of yours to see you.

He goes out quickly, and the two women are left looking at each other.

Quick Curtain

SCENE TWO

*It is a few minutes later. From Cliff's room, across the
landing, comes the sound of Jimmy's jazz trumpet. At rise of
the Curtain, Helena is standing L of the table, pouring out a
cup of tea. Alison is sitting on the armchair R. She bends
down and picks up Jimmy's pipe. Then she scoops up a little
pile of ash from the floor, and drops it in the ashtray on the
arm of the chair.*

Alison He still smokes this foul old stuff. I used to hate it at
first, but you get used to it.

Helena Yes.

Alison I went to the pictures last week, and some old man
was smoking it in front, a few rows away. I actually got up,
and sat right behind him.

Helena (*coming down with cup of tea*) Here, have this. It
usually seems to help.

Alison (*taking it*) Thanks.

Helena Are you sure you feel all right now?

Alison (*nods*) It was just – oh, everything. It's my own fault –
entirely. I must be mad, coming here like this. I'm sorry,
Helena.

Helena Why should you be sorry – you of all people?

Alison Because it was unfair and cruel of me to come back.
I'm afraid a sense of timing is one of the things I seem to have
learnt from Jimmy. But it's something that can be in very bad
taste. (*sips her tea*) So many times, I've just managed to stop
myself coming here – right at the last moment. Even today,
when I went to the booking office at St Pancras, it was like a
charade, and I never believed that I'd let myself walk on to
that train. And when I was on it, I got into a panic. I felt like

a criminal. I told myself I'd turn round at the other end, and come straight back. I couldn't even believe that this place existed any more. But once I got here, there was nothing I could do. I had to convince myself that everything I remembered about this place had really happened to me once. (*She lowers her cup, and her foot plays with the newspapers on the floor.*) How many times in these past few months I've thought of the evenings we used to spend here in this room. Suspended and rather remote. You make a good cup of tea.

Helena (*sitting L of table*) Something Jimmy taught *me*.

Alison (*covering her face*) Oh, why am I here! You must all wish me a thousand miles away!

Helena I don't wish anything of the kind. You've more right to be here than I.

Alison Oh, Helena, don't bring out the book of rules –

Helena You are his wife, aren't you? Whatever I have done, I've never been able to forget that fact. You have all the rights –

Alison Helena – even I gave up believing in the divine rights of marriage long ago. Even before I met Jimmy. They've got something different now – constitutional monarchy. You are where you are by consent. And if you start trying any strong arm stuff, you're out. And I'm out.

Helena Is that something you learnt from him?

Alison Don't make me feel like a blackmailer or something, please! I've done something foolish, and rather vulgar in coming here tonight. I regret it, and I detest myself for doing it. But I did not come here in order to gain anything. Whatever it was – hysteria or just macabre curiosity, I'd certainly no intention of making any kind of breach between you and Jimmy. You must believe that.

94

Helena Oh, I believe it all right. That's why everything seems more wrong and terrible than ever. You didn't even reproach me. You should have been outraged, but you weren't. (*She leans back, as if she wanted to draw back from herself.*) I feel so – *ashamed.*

Alison You talk as though he were something you'd swindled me out of –

Helena (*fiercely*) And you talk as if he were a book or something you pass around to anyone who happens to want it for five minutes. What's the matter with you? You sound as though you were quoting *him* all the time. I thought you told me once you couldn't bring yourself to believe in him.

Alison I don't think I ever believed in your way either.

Helena At least, I still believe in right and wrong! Not even the months in this madhouse have stopped me doing that. Even though everything I have done is wrong, at least I have known it was wrong.

Alison You loved him, didn't you? That's what you wrote and told me.

Helena And it was true.

Alison It was pretty difficult to believe at the time. I couldn't understand it.

Helena I could hardly believe it myself.

Alison Afterwards, it wasn't quite so difficult. You used to say some pretty harsh things about him. Not that I was sorry to hear them – they were rather comforting then. But you even shocked me sometimes.

Helena I suppose I was a little over-emphatic. There doesn't seem much point in trying to explain everything, does there?

Alison Not really.

Helena Do you know – I have discovered what is wrong with Jimmy? It's very simple really. He was born out of his time.

Alison Yes. I know.

Helena There's no place for people like that any longer – in sex, or politics, or anything. That's why he's so futile. Sometimes, when I listen to him, I feel he thinks he's still in the middle of the French Revolution. And that's where he ought to be, of course. He doesn't know where he is, or where he's going. He'll never do anything, and he'll never amount to anything.

Alison I suppose he's what you'd call an Eminent Victorian. Slightly comic – in a way . . . We seem to have had this conversation before.

Helena Yes, I remember everything you said about him. It horrified me. I couldn't believe that you could have married someone like that. Alison – it's all over between Jimmy and me. I can see it now. I've got to get out. No – listen to me. When I saw you standing there tonight, I knew that it was all utterly wrong. That I didn't believe in any of this, and not Jimmy or anyone could make me believe otherwise. (*rising*) How could I have ever thought I could get away with it! He wants one world and I want another, and lying in that bed won't ever change it! I believe in good and evil, and I don't have to apologize for that. It's quite a modern, scientific belief now, so they tell me. And, by everything I have ever believed in, or wanted, what I have been doing is wrong and evil.

Alison Helena – you're not going to leave him?

Helena Yes, I am. (*Before Alison can interrupt, she goes on.*) Oh, I'm not stepping aside to let you come back. You can do what you like. Frankly, I think you'd be a fool – but that's your own business. I think I've given you enough advice.

Alison But he – he'll have no one.

Helena Oh, my dear, he'll find somebody. He'll probably hold court here like one of the Renaissance popes. Oh, I know I'm throwing the book of rules at you, as you call it, but, believe me, you're never going to be happy without it. I tried throwing it away all these months, but I know now it just doesn't work. When you came in at that door, ill and tired and hurt, it was all over for me. You see – I didn't know about the baby. It was such a shock. It's like a judgment on us.

Alison You saw me, and I had to tell you what had happened. I lost the child. It's a simple fact. There is no judgment, there's no blame –

Helena Maybe not. But I feel it just the same.

Alison But don't you see? It isn't logical!

Helena No, it isn't. (*calmly*) But I know it's right.

The trumpet gets louder.

Alison Helena, (*going to her*) you mustn't leave him. He needs you, I know he needs you –

Helena Do you think so?

Alison Maybe you're not the right one for him – we're neither of us right –

Helena (*moving upstage*) Oh, why doesn't he stop that damned noise!

Alison He wants something quite different from us. What it is exactly I don't know – a kind of cross between a mother and a Greek courtesan, a henchwoman, a mixture of Cleopatra and Boswell. But give him a little longer –

Helena (*wrenching the door open*) Please! Will you stop that! I can't think!

There is a slight pause, and the trumpet goes on. She puts her hands on her head.

Jimmy, for God's sake!

It stops.

Jimmy, I want to speak to you.

Jimmy (*off*) Is your friend still with you?

Helena Oh, don't be an idiot, and come in here! (*She moves down L.*)

Alison (*rising*) He doesn't want to see me.

Helena Stay where you are, and don't be silly. I'm sorry. It won't be very pleasant, but I've made up my mind to go, and I've got to tell him now.

Enter Jimmy.

Jimmy Is this another of your dark plots? (*He looks at Alison.*) Hadn't she better sit down? She looks a bit ghastly.

Helena I'm so sorry, dear. Would you like some more tea, or an aspirin or something?

Alison shakes her head, and sits. She can't look at either of them.

(*to Jimmy, the old authority returning*) It's not very surprising, is it? She's been very ill, she's –

Jimmy (*quietly*) You don't have to draw a diagram for me – I can see what's happened to her.

Helena And doesn't it mean anything to you?

Jimmy I don't exactly relish the idea of anyone being ill, or in pain. It was my child too, you know. But (*he shrugs*) it isn't my first loss.

Alison (*on her breath*) It was mine.

He glances at her, but turns back to Helena quickly.

98

Jimmy What are you looking so solemn about? What's she doing here?

Alison I'm sorry, I'm – (*Presses her hand over her mouth.*)

Helena crosses to Jimmy C, and grasps his hand.

Helena Don't please. Can't you see the condition she's in? She's done nothing, she's said nothing, none of it's her fault.

He takes his hand away, and moves away a little downstage.

Jimmy What isn't her fault?

Helena Jimmy – I don't want a brawl, so please –

Jimmy Let's hear it, shall we?

Helena Very well. I'm going downstairs to pack my things. If I hurry, I shall just catch the 7.15 to London.

They both look at him, but he simply leans forward against the table, not looking at either of them.

This is not Alison's doing – you must understand that. It's my own decision entirely. In fact, she's just been trying to talk me out of it. It's just that suddenly, tonight, I see what I have really known all along. That you can't be happy when what you're doing is wrong, or is hurting someone else. I suppose it could never have worked, anyway, but I do love you, Jimmy. I shall never love anyone as I have loved you. (*turns away L*) But I can't go on. (*passionately and sincerely*) I can't take part – in all this suffering. I can't!

She appeals to him for some reaction, but he only looks down at the table, and nods. Helena recovers, and makes an effort to regain authority.

(*to Alison*) You probably won't feel up to making that journey again tonight, but we can fix you up at an hotel before I go. There's about half an hour. I'll just make it.

She turns up to the door, but Jimmy's voice stops her.

Jimmy (*in a low, resigned voice*) They all want to escape from the pain of being alive. And, most of all, from love. (*crosses to the dressing table*) I always knew something like this would turn up – some problem, like an ill wife – and it would be too much for those delicate hot-house feelings of yours.

He sweeps up Helena's things from the dressing table, and crosses over to the wardrobe. Outside, the church bells start ringing.

It's no good trying to fool yourself about love. You can't fall into it like a soft job, without dirtying up your hands. (*He hands her the make-up things, which she takes. He opens the wardrobe.*) It takes muscle and guts. And if you can't bear the thought (*takes out a dress on a hanger*) of messing up your nice, clean soul (*crossing back to her*) you'd better give up the whole idea of life, and become a saint. (*He puts the dress in her arms.*) Because you'll never make it as a human being. It's either this world or the next.

She looks at him for a moment, and then goes out quickly. He is shaken, and he avoids Alison's eyes, crossing to the window. He rests against it, then bangs his fist against the frame.

Oh, those bells!

The shadows are growing around them. Jimmy stands, his head against the window pane. Alison is huddled forward in the armchair R. Presently, she breaks the stillness, and rises to above the table.

Alison I'm . . . sorry. I'll go now.

She starts to move upstage. But his voice pulls her up.

Jimmy You never even sent any flowers to the funeral. Not –

a little bunch of flowers. You had to deny me that too, didn't you?

She starts to move, but again he speaks.

The injustice of it is almost perfect! The wrong people going hungry, the wrong people being loved, the wrong people dying!

She moves to the gas stove. He turns to face her.

Was I really wrong to believe that there's a – a kind of – burning virility of mind and spirit that looks for something as powerful as itself? The heaviest, strongest creatures in this world seem to be the loneliest. Like the old bear, following his own breath in the dark forest. There's no warm pack, no herd to comfort him. That voice that cries out doesn't *have* to be a weakling's, does it? (*He moves in a little.*) Do you remember that first night I saw you at that grisly party? You didn't really notice me, but I was watching you all the evening. You seemed to have a wonderful relaxation of spirit. I knew that was what I wanted. You've got to be really brawny to have that kind of strength – the strength to relax. It was only after we were married that I discovered that it wasn't relaxation at all. In order to relax, you've first got to sweat your guts out. And, as far as you were concerned, you'd never had a hair out of place, or a bead of sweat anywhere.

A cry escapes from her, and her fist flies to her mouth. She moves down to below the table, leaning on it.

I may be a lost cause, but I thought if you loved me, it needn't matter.

She is crying silently. He moves down to face her.

Alison It doesn't matter! I was wrong, I was wrong! I don't want to be neutral, I don't want to be a saint. I want to be a lost cause. I want to be corrupt and futile!

All he can do is watch her helplessly. Her voice takes on a little strength, and rises.

Don't you understand? It's gone! It's gone! That – that helpless human being inside my body. I thought it was so safe, and secure in there. Nothing could take it from me. It was mine, my responsibility. But it's lost. (*She slides down against the leg of the table to the floor.*) All I wanted was to die. I never knew what it was like. I didn't know it could be like that! I was in pain, and all I could think of was you, and what I'd lost. (*scarcely able to speak*) I thought: if only – if only he could see me now, so stupid, and ugly and ridiculous. This is what he's been longing for me to feel. This is what he wants to splash about in! I'm in the fire, and I'm burning, and all I want is to die! It's cost him his child, and any others I might have had! But what does it matter – this is what he wanted from me!

She raises her face to him.

Don't you see! I'm in the mud at last! I'm grovelling! I'm crawling! Oh, God –

She collapses at his feet. He stands, frozen for a moment, then he bends down and takes her shaking body in his arms. He shakes his head, and whispers:

Jimmy Don't. Please don't . . . I can't –

She gasps for her breath against him.

You're all right. You're all right now. Please, I – I . . . Not any more . . .

She relaxes suddenly. He looks down at her, full of fatigue, and says with a kind of mocking, tender irony:

We'll be together in our bear's cave, and our squirrel's drey, and we'll live on honey, and nuts – lots and lots of nuts. And we'll sing songs about ourselves – about warm trees and snug caves, and lying in the sun. And you'll keep those big eyes on my fur, and help me keep my claws in order, because I'm a bit of a soppy, scruffy sort of a bear. And I'll see that you keep that sleek, bushy tail glistening as it should, because you're a very beautiful squirrel, but you're none too bright either, so we've got to be careful. There are cruel steel traps lying about everywhere, just waiting for rather mad, slightly satanic, and very timid little animals. Right?

Alison nods.

(*pathetically*) Poor squirrels!

Alison (*with the same comic emphasis*) Poor bears! (*She laughs a little. Then looks at him very tenderly, and adds very, very softly.*) Oh, poor, poor bears!

Slides her arms around him.

Afterword

I Have a Go, Lady, I Have a Go

This was the inaugural John Osborne lecture, given at the Hay-on-Wye Literary Festival in June 2002 in the presence of his widow, Helen, and not far from the home on the Welsh borders where they spent the last years of their lives.

I don't see how any British playwright could be more honoured than to be asked to speak in public in memory of John Osborne. Just to invoke John's name and to recall the nature of his endeavour is to plug yourself straight into the main supply, the feeding house, the grid that makes our local culture spark and fizz. Here it comes again: the myth of the playwright who will seek to drive a straight line towards the heart of his or her own subject matter; the dramatist, educated in the playhouse not at the university, who will be neither academic and obscure on the one hand, nor stupid and populist on the other. Here they are once more, the playwrights who disdain pretension, false high-mindedness and didacticism, who won't talk down and who won't gussy up; these are the writers who don't want an art theatre or a theatre of snobs, who can't see a future in the etiolated antics of self-referential up-your-bum experimentalism, and yet who also refuse to set fallible audiences up – just people, after all – as the only or ultimate judges of their work, and who therefore aren't prepared to grovel and fawn in the cause of their amusement. Welcome instead to an ideal of theatre founded in recognition: spectators charged up by the presentation of their own lives, sitting in the dark, sometimes openly resentful, sometimes openly thrilled at the experience of confronting their own, often shameful, often dangerous feelings. Say the name 'John Osborne' and stick your fingers, as you longed to as a child, straight into the socket. Stick them in and sizzle.

It is an inevitable drawback of this, the first memorial lecture in John's name, that a period of seventy-three years after a writer's birth and of just eight after his early death offers perhaps the worst possible platform from which to give an intelligent account of a man's life and work. We are at the wrong distance. The German poet Rainer Maria Rilke called fame 'the sum of all misunderstandings which collects about a name'. Since it was John's great fortune to enjoy the most celebrated theatrical début of the twentieth century, so his misfortune has been consequently to attract some of its laziest and worst-aimed critical animus. There is a general feeling around that because John was never seen to be overly nervous of dishing it out, so there is no reason why he shouldn't also be given some. As in the case of Orson Welles, John's early acclaim has made the story of his life all too convenient a parable of squandered promise. What's the point of a myth if you can't de-bunk it? 'Misogynist', 'little Englander', 'embittered Edwardian', 'hopeless misanthrope', 'Garrick club member' are a few of the cheerless epithets retrospectively slung around in an effort to discredit the originality of the man who lies in a grave in a Clun churchyard, on the border between England and Wales.

No one can mistake the purpose underlying most of the attempts to talk John down. Under the pious expressions of disappointment, the seen-it-all head-shaking over a career begun in such high hope, lies a far more insidious, far more political project. Clearly, a fashionable need exists, for reasons which we shall in a few minutes try to explore, to attempt to deny the meaning of a moment which has admittedly passed too easily into history. Behind the desire to belittle John and to belittle John's work lies a much more urgent agenda. The plan, clearly, is to challenge the myth of 1956 and what it is feared to represent in British culture. This, let us remind ourselves, was the establishment, by the force of a single play, written by a man who only one year earlier had been touring as Freddy Eynsford Hill in a deadbeat production of *Pygmalion*, of a principled new play venue in Sloane Square. The Royal Court, as conceived by George Devine, was to be a theatre committed to the uncommon notion, to this day both revolutionary and banal, that at the centre of all great dramatic adventure belongs the unpredictable, uncompromising figure of the living playwright.

'The hero has a sweet stall,' said Noël Coward, when, at the age of fifty-seven, the old rogue came down from his hilltop in Jamaica and for the first time admitted to having read *Look Back in Anger*. 'I should like to know, given his passion for invective, how the hero manages to sell any sweets.' There is in that tone of oh-so-English put-down at least, mercifully, a simulacrum of style, the remains of a world-attitude, however feeble, however dated. But the trend-spotters of our own generation who, at the outset of the twenty-first century, line up eagerly to argue that the controversy raging around John's first performed play was all some kind of ghastly mistake, do not even pretend to any thoughtful view of why the work itself might once have triggered such astonishing contemporary passion. For them, the play's existence, and the reputation it carries of henceforward rooting most of what is outstanding in British fiction in the performing arts, are offence enough. Many people cannot bear the idea that a work of art can once have existed which conveyed so much power and effect. Their vision of living theatre is still best expressed in Robert Morley's timeless manifesto: 'All that English audiences need, deserve or want is me and Noël in terrible plays written by ourselves.'

In this modern atmosphere of spiteful revisionism – which now marks our politics as much as it does our culture; few people, God knows, wanting to be caught out looking remotely excited – it has sadly become necessary before speaking of any exceptional event to make clear what it is you are *not* saying before you go on to risk saying anything at all. When today I insist on the special qualities of *Look Back in Anger* and on its author's subsequent contribution to an interesting piece of English social history, then let me make clear that I am not thereby intending any implicit discourtesy to anyone else. To spell it out: I am not saying that, if you like that sort of thing, Christopher Fry was not a jolly good playwright; I am not saying that in her radical work at Stratford East Joan Littlewood was not a specific kind of English genius, gifted with a restless, fecund directorial inventiveness which this spectator has not seen matched since; I am not saying that Rodney Ackland did not, in the rush and hurry of new-wave agitation, get criminally overlooked in the late agonising years of his life; and I am not even saying that it is technically impossible to write a great play in which, for all I know, heroes and heroines burst with unbearable force through French windows, naked below the knee, bearing high-tensile tennis rackets, and with them, themes of shattering symbolic and spiritual

108

importance. Given the right author, it may very well be. Stranger things go on in the name of entertainment. But I *am* insisting, however, that John did something almost unique. He reconnected the British theatre urgently to its audience, and he spread its influence way beyond its regular habitués and fans.

Again, in celebrating the genuine impact of this one play, it is essential to make clear that I am not describing something which we would today experience as a familiar piece of media contrivance. By chance, it was my own fate to end up as the author of one of the more publicised stage plays of the last fifty years when Sam Mendes asked me to adapt Schnitzler's scenes, *Reigen*, never intended for performance, and to re-set them in the present day, allowing only two actors to take the ten roles. When *Newsweek*, all smoky blues and flesh-tones, decided to forgo current events and pseudo-science and instead to splash Nicole Kidman in fishnet tights to herald the play's New York opening, then it was believed to be the first time that an American news magazine had thought a mere stage play worthy of its cover since the zenith of Tennessee Williams. But never for a moment did Sam, Nicole or I confuse a modern electronic sandstorm with either significance or reverberation. The three of us knew that *The Blue Room* was an innocent freak, mostly a freak of publicity. It was, in our eyes, a subtle and unsettling small-scale play, more tender than its reputation, which had somehow been picked up by the wind and taken for something it wasn't. Enemies of John Osborne like to pretend that the events surrounding his play were parallel: the first modern example, they say, of journalistic hype bringing a weight down on a play which it could not possibly carry.

The reply to this charge is best found in a performance of the play itself. When *Look Back in Anger* was well revived at the National Theatre only a few years ago, and unleashed from its original social context – for those of us who lived through them as infants, the memorably deadly early 1950s – then it seemed not at all the typically English play best known for initiating a supposed sea-change in English theatre. On the contrary – and most especially in the eyes of the foreigner sitting beside me – it seemed a defiantly foreign work; perhaps even a rogue, a sport, a one-off. 'Where did *this* one come from?' asked my neighbour. She could see no ancestry. She, like me, had been watching a Strindbergian account of a domestic relationship, which feels richer than Strindberg for being layered with a knowledge of events outside the little room, for managing to imply the desolating movement of history, but which is also burning up emotionally with a most un-English intensity. For those of us still shaken by the events on stage, it seemed clearer than ever that John's trilogy of *Look Back in Anger*, *The Entertainer* and *Inadmissible Evidence* are not important for what they are said to have removed from the English stage – good taste, irony, deflection, lame jokes, and rigidly chewed upper lips – but revolutionary for what everyone now forgets they put in their place. I mean strong feeling.

'Yes, but what are you angry *about*?' It was, John said, the question he was most frequently asked – or rather, the second most frequent after, 'How much money have you made out of all this?' 'The English hate energy,' said one of the Royal Court's directors, Lindsay Anderson, who noted that no sooner had a new kind of drama begun at last to appear than the press rushed to give it the name 'kitchen sink', in an effort to patronise it, contain it and kill it with the easiest instrument to hand – the convenient English weapon of class. The legend tells us that when the curtain went up on that evening in May 1956, the audience gasped at the sight of an ironing board. More likely, they gasped at the sound of the words. For years, critics had been anticipating a poetic revival, and had turned their faces to the finer publishing houses of Bloomsbury for some stick-dry, crackle-breathed English poet to mimic the Elizabethans in the playhouse. In fact, when poetry did burst gloriously over the stage, it came, as always, from a direction which nobody was expecting: from the mouth of a provincial trumpet-player, a malcontent, a cad.

(It is worth adding in parentheses that the second likely reason for its exceptional impact was that *Look Back in Anger* was the first English play for many decades to be so clearly rooted in the pleasures of bed. Why else was Kenneth Tynan so immediately enthused by it? The play appeared at a moment when approved theatre, as represented by Coward, Eliot and J. B. Priestley, glowed with an erotic charge somewhat less than a forty-watt bulb. Then John Osborne arrives, childish or child-like according to your point of view, but anyway blessed with a D. H. Lawrence-like conviction that people can't be known or understood except through the act of love. The character of Helena – the woman who affects to despise Jimmy Porter, but who longs to sleep with him – is there to remind you that bed will be the only crucible in which true feeling is revealed and put to the test. My God, no wonder hackles went up, stayed up, and have never really been taken down.)

The American pop historian Greil Marcus records that when Elvis Presley went into the army, had his hair cut and was posted to Germany, Marcus's first, unspoken feeling was one of intense, shaming relief. To a boy growing up in the US heartland Elvis rampant had been an almost unbearable threat. Obviously, like everyone else, you had to *say* you liked him – you had to follow the script and *profess* to like him – but secretly you were scared stiff. Elvis's gyrating hips, the insane sexuality and throb of his music, the public example of someone managing at once to be both so rebellious and so impossibly cool, seemed to bring home to the young Marcus everything that he himself was missing in his life, and implicitly therefore, in his character. If Elvis could be like this, then why couldn't you? You had no one to blame but yourself. The young knew that a gauntlet was being thrown down. And some of them also knew that they were both terrified and inadequate to pick it up. When the state got hold of Elvis and conscripted him, it was conscripting energy itself. When they proved that no one can survive for long in show business without being packaged into just one more nice American mother's boy – later, one more nice American mother's boy with the defining avoirdupois of the species – then Marcus pretended – again like everyone else – to be let down and cheated by his one-time hero. But inside, he felt other.

I have no doubt that, in a similar way, British resentment of *Look Back in Anger*, and recent attempts to rewrite its place in history, are, finally, resentment of vitality. One way or another, the bald can't wait for Samson to get a trim. Those expressions of disappointment about John's later work are, in fact, disguised expressions of gratitude that his challenge was not sustained. The eventual fall-out between the critic who first championed the playwright's work and the playwright himself was both necessary and inevitable. A tide of gossip has always washed over Kenneth Tynan's ambivalent relationship with John – fan and fan-object – but gossip misses the point that their deepest disagreement was about theatre itself. In Tynan's eloquent admiration for what he called 'high-definition performance' you find what is fundamentally a worship of skill, of technique, of expertise, and implicitly therefore of success. In Osborne's values, you find a love of emotion, of high, true, uncensored feeling, of human weakness and therefore of failure. It was unlikely the two men were going to get on for very long. At the end of his life, Ken was left watching Shirley Maclaine and Marlene Dietrich. At the end of his, John was left reading *The Book of Common Prayer*.

'It is not the business of writers to accuse or to prosecute,' wrote the nineteenth century's greatest playwright. 'We have enough accusers, prosecutors and gendarmes without them.' This typically affable statement by Chekhov, on the surface so restful, so accommodating, so magnanimously fair, would make more sense to us and probably ring a good deal truer if we had not actually seen Chekhov's own plays, especially the younger ones. For all their fabulous likeability, these plays are, underneath, more unsparing of human failings than those of any dramatist I know. If, like the rest of us, you suffer from any hidden flaw which you might wish to conceal in your otherwise impeccable character, then the individual in all history with whom I would least recommend a relaxing weekend is a certain bearded Russian physician, anointed by his less discerning admirers with the word 'humane'. Your chances of driving away on Monday morning with your strategies of disguise intact I would rate as nil. It is precisely this quality, the ability to see through everyone, and most of all, to see through one's own pathetic fabrications, which marks out some of our most searching dramatists. (Such writers choose theatre because theatre is scrutiny.) And I suspect it is this quality – call it a certain ruthlessness of eye – which John's critics most distrust.

'It's hard,' suggests Christopher Hampton, in unlikely praise of Noël Coward, 'not to like a man who wrote, towards the end of his life, "I don't look back in anger, nor indeed in anything approaching mild rage; I rather look back with pleasure and amusement."' For my own part, when I think of Coward, I have to stick pins in my palms to remember not to despise him. Coward's great limitation as a playwright – and at once the source of his considerable comedy – is his determination to leave people as archetypes. He seals off their faults, letting them go by, as if they are just the traits people are born with, and about which they can do very little. 'Hey-ho,' as he would say. John's opposing instinct is to get things out in the open, to dig down and to look deep, to forgive no one, least of all himself. In his most popular work, *Private Lives*, Coward argues openly, and with the air of a man who believes that insouciance is a moral virtue, that it doesn't much matter what we do on earth because we're all going to die. It would be hard to imagine a philosophy more alien to John's. Underlying every word Osborne wrote is a rather different conviction. Because we are all going to die, it is therefore extremely important what we do now.

John's subject is, essentially, failure. John brings you news of what it is like not to succeed, to know you are not succeeding, either with yourself or with others – ever seen an Osborne hero with a dry brow? – and he does it in a medium in which the reality of failure is always more painful, more present than in any other. Why is John angry? Why are Bill Maitland, Archie Rice and Jimmy Porter angry? Because the chances of realising our dreams are so few, and the possibility is that, even so, we will miss our chances when they come. John is our poet laureate of flopsweat, of lost opportunity, of missed connections and of hidden dread, of what he himself calls 'the comfortless tragedy of isolated hearts'. John's plays are what you feel when you wake prickling in the dark: half-truth experienced as whole truth, intuition experienced as fact. John's characters, quivering, vibrating with life, have no clue how to put the nightmare away, how to chuck it, forget it, put a sock in it, repress it or even, for God's sake, how to talk the bloody thing to death. These are people to whom the fear always returns.

In retrospect, at what I earlier described as an inconvenient distance, I believe we can begin to see John as part of a rich generation of dramatic writers, whose prescience in the face of the arrival of a pervasive consumer society was to make a hugely romantic gesture of defiance in defence of the individual. Whether they were consciously political or not – and John, let's face it, could never make up his mind – these writers shared, in a broad way, a common analysis. In their view, the loss of an imperial role had sent the British into a period of painful self-ignorance. Boasting a ridiculous bomb they plainly could not use, and an international influence they plainly did not have, the leaders of our island race were behaving like embarrassing twits, while the people themselves appeared – in the public prints, at least – to be interested only in becoming paid-up members of the affluent society as fast as they possibly could. The novel in England, Doris Lessing honourably apart, had already turned its back on historical and social questions and gone into the dull slump of mindless solipsism from which it has never recovered. (To this day, you have to look to America – *Catch 22*, *The Catcher in the Rye*, *The Corrections* – for novels which reach out directly to influence people's lives; here, it is always going to be films, TV and theatre – *The Boys from the Blackstuff*, *Cathy Come Home*, *Look Back in Anger*.) And so it fell to the stage playwrights to mark out a vital patch of territory.

When they were alive, you would probably have felt that many things separated the sensibilities of writers as disparate as David Mercer, Dennis Potter and John Osborne. One, after all, was a painter and a Marxist; the second was a journalist and a Labour candidate; the third an actor and – well, a sort of faltering patriot. But as time passes, and what we lived through and just called 'life' is slowly seen to be history, so what these men – and yes, they were all men – had in common stands out more clearly. In each one of them you find a stubborn, ornery determination not to let themselves or other people be blanded into oblivion. What they have in common is what John himself called a delight in 'going too far'. Only by going too far, said John, could performed work begin to move into a place where unease in the audience becomes creative, where that funny meltdown happens when you no longer know what you think. When Dennis Potter makes sure to alert us, in at least five of his plays, I reckon, to his own predilection for, and fascination with, prostitution; or when David Mercer, haunted by the examples of heroism in Eastern Europe, rails in flailing, drunken incoherence at the horror of remaining in the West, useless but alive; or when John, to the shock of all right-thinking people, judges it an autobiographical imperative to tell us of his desire to gob, like a passing bird, on his ex-wife's open coffin, then all three writers reveal a shared, underlying purpose. Their aim is always to hang on, to insist on what is dark, what is peculiar, what is disturbing – let me put it the way they would like me to put it: to hang on to what is *true* – in the face of what they fear to be the coming homogenisation of everything.

It will be obvious even to those of you not lucky enough to have met these three men in their prime that none of them was what you would describe as easy company. With each of them, I had at times variously difficult evenings. If we accept Flaubert's perfect definition of what one needs to get through life unscathed – 'To be stupid, selfish and have good health are the three requirements of happiness, though if stupidity is lacking, all is lost' – then we can see that for three such emotionally intelligent human beings, the battle for any easeful passage was probably lost before it was begun. And yet to someone of my upbringing, coming as I did from a quite different background and with quite different assumptions about what was happening in the 1960s, there was something almost bewilderingly masochistic about my seniors – writers perhaps ten or twenty years older – as if, sometimes, none of them were able to disentangle their profound and real hatred of what was happening to society with their much more shocking hatred of what was happening inside them. Who was the enemy here? Society or yourself? When my own play *Teeth 'n' Smiles* was presented at the Royal Court and widely greeted as the work of a new John Osborne – he'd done the music hall, I was doing rock 'n' roll – then I was flattered but confused. By quirk, I have as little sense of my own literary provenance as I do of the individual cow that provided my shoes, or the particular sheep that died for my supper. For me, deep influence is always un-conscious. But it seemed axiomatic that I could have little in common with a writer whose priorities were, by then, so obviously different from my own.

Again, looking back, it is an odd paradox that my own gifted contemporaries – let's say, at least for the sake of argument, Howard Brenton, Howard Barker, Caryl Churchill, David Edgar and Trevor Griffiths – were greeted in the broadsheets as though they were the devil in hell, when they were, in person, so much more easy-going than their immediate predecessors. In Argentina, the Shakespeare comedy *Much Ado About Nothing* is given under the far snappier title *Much Noise, Few Nuts*. *Much Noise, Few Nuts* sums up pretty well the value of nearly all middle-aged critical reaction to the arrival of fresh life in the arts. When Bernard Levin used to launch his humourless, knotty philippics against a pack of play-wrights who, he claimed, were intent on destroying civi-lisation itself (all served up in that atrociously contrived prose which more gullible parts of the *Times* readership used to mistake for style) then I would just laugh and wonder what would happen if Levin actually met any of my peers. Whatever personal torture and agony may have marked our private lives, we did not see it as part of our mission directly to display our individual souls on the stage. We felt we were putting just as much sweat, feeling and passion into our work, but it was clearly im-portant to the exercise that romantic agony should not, for our purpose, necessarily show. (As William Empson put it, 'The careless ease always goes in last.') Whereas the generation before us were involved in a no-holds-barred defence of the individual, in which self-exposure, self-excoriation and even self-annihilation were regular ingredients, we, in our beginnings at least, were much more concerned to tell stories which might offer some equally passionate defence of the collective.

These were, I suppose, the only two sensible responses in the second half of the twentieth century to the sudden collapse of confidence in the West's sense of itself. You could either, as it were, regroup and insist that the duty of the writer was, at all times, to remind people that the human soul was deeper and darker than the countless numbing strategies of advertising and business – and of their outpost, Fleet Street – were planning to represent it. Or else you could assert, in the face of sometimes formidable evidence to the contrary, that the lot of human beings was still improvable. It seemed obvious to us: the pervasive feeling of national despair was not existential, but organisational. What we were lacking was not self-knowledge, but social justice. Whereas the collapse of the empire, the invention of the nuclear bomb and the brutality of Stalinism defined the thinking of people a little older than us, so the murderous war crimes of the Americans in Vietnam, the failure of social democracy under Harold Wilson and the continuing threat actually to use that terrible bomb marked our own. The achievement of a writer like Howard Brenton was to find unexpected comedy in the left's everyday passion for progress; the corresponding achievement of Trevor Griffiths was to compare the diamond-hard fervour of the past with the left's wavering accommodations of the present.

There is little, in this context, to add about my own plays, except to observe that I could not, for the life of me, work out why there were so few women on the stage that I had inherited. It seemed self-evident that an art form which sought to represent life could not be doing its job as long as it disallowed more or less half the human race from a position anywhere near the centre of the stage. I was aware, naturally, that most of my contemporaries had already abandoned the idea of the leading role. They saw it as invidious. Writers like Caryl Churchill chose to express exhilarating ideas through the movement of the group, and rarely through the articulation of a single individual: the Osborne tradition. Sometimes I designed plays for an ensemble of twenty-five, but when I also wrote the parts which were played by Kate Nelligan in *Knuckle* and in *Licking Hitler*, by Kate Nelligan and Meryl Streep in *Plenty*, by Helen Mirren in *Teeth 'n' Smiles*, by Irene Worth in *The Bay at Nice*, and later by Judi Dench in *Amy's View*, then I was conscious of deliberately persisting in a practice which some people felt made nonsense of my politics. Why should one person have all the lines? I felt the contrary. Why should the contradictions of society – we live in contradiction, breathe it, swim in it – not be as powerfully expressed by one person as by many?

Clearly it remains a matter of historical record that the strategies of all our liveliest writers, whether of the left or of the right, were put in a new and unflattering perspective by the rise of a 1980s social movement which left many dramatists, and indeed the theatre itself, looking both weak and sanctimonious against an onset of energy to which it initially had little response. When global capitalism fired up its engines, freed up its markets, kicked up a gear and assumed its historic destiny of infinitely enriching the rich and further impoverishing the poor, then, for a while, culture stood on the kerb, like a vicar whose cassock has been splashed by a passing Maserati. None of us distinguished ourselves by the speed with which we responded to what was happening. A commercial producer requested me to cut the word 'capitalism'. 'Audiences,' he said, 'don't like it.' 'OK,' I said, 'so what should I call it instead?' 'Oh,' he said, 'just call it life.'

We had all assumed for so long that the injustices of a particular system would somehow lead to some sort of reckoning, however crude, however violent, that everyone was rendered speechless when the system renewed itself from within. Mercer died suddenly, aged fifty-two – in Israel, as it happens, so he was buried in a British military cemetery, on the main road just outside Haifa. His last work was titled *No Limits to Love*. Potter started scouring his memories of the Forest of Dean, in search of terrain on which he might feel more at home. Just before his death, in a statement which summed up attitudes held in common by many writers of his age, he observed: 'For me, religion is not the bandage, it's the wound.' And John Osborne responded to the ubiquity of the present by retreating into the past. His volumes of theatrical memoir, which rank with Moss Hart's as the best ever written, fortify the myth of a golden age, a Utopia of memory in which George Devine is forever pacing the upper circle of the Royal Court, and in which girls, maybe a little squiffy, are forever waiting, with lipstick, bobs, short skirts and cigarettes in bars on the outer reaches of Chelsea or Manhattan.

Naturally, I cannot pretend that during these years of John's failing impact as a dramatist I felt wholly in tune with his predicaments. Other people's problems always look so much easier than your own. As a young man to whom the toolkit of politics was always ready in the garage to deal with random human breakdown, it seemed briefly obvious that if you based your defence of humanity on the personal pronoun, on the 'I' that is within us all, the 'I' that screams '*I* am unusual, *I* am valuable,' then you may soon find yourself more and more contemplating a painted view of a time and a place when that 'I' found perfect self-expression. Surely the word 'integrity' had to mean more than 'truth to myself'? John's comic fulminations against the arbitrary groupings that grew to attract his dislike no longer seemed to represent the strong, deep, true feeling he had once conveyed. Instead he was forced back into a position which, finally, for most writers is both undignified and unproductive: the pretence that the past is always, necessarily, superior to the present. We had passed from passion to prejudice. Sometimes it appeared as if the moment of his own projectile heat had been so great, and so greatly defining, he could no longer find warmth anywhere else. In his last years, he appeared like the owner of a huge, peeling seaside villa, in which great parties had once been held. In his writing, he occasionally became careless of Duke Ellington's great injunction: 'Never forget: chords may be our love, but rhythm is our business.'

To be fair, life was not proving any easier for the rest of us. My favourite moment in Trotsky's writings comes when the great thinker demonstrates a fallible grasp of the American cultural scene by addressing his remarks to 'the workers and peasants of the South Bronx'. Those of us who had set out intending to address the workers and peasants of the British theatregoing community sometimes looked scarcely less silly. I certainly refused to cut the word 'capitalism' – always will refuse to cut it: capitalism *isn't* life – but even so, with Western society apparently charging off in an unforeseen direction, you would have had to have been one of Flaubert's happy idiots not to be aware of how hard it was to work in the traditional arts and not look ridiculous. In my world, it became expedient to say that it was no longer possible to write a play which would affect society's temperature, because society itself, the media and the West's love affair with mocking self-irony had reached a point where only decorative art could speak to large numbers. People wanted chopped sharks they could look at, not words they would actually have to think about. It was claimed that the moral arts were a bust. I thought this unlikely. If there was no modern *Look Back in Anger*, then the probable reason was that none of us were good enough to write it. For me, the aim of writing it, or rather, the aim of reproducing its effect, remains a timeless ideal.

Those who opposed John, and what John wished the British theatre to become, tend rightly to point out that nothing he stood for has come to pass. In support of their argument for his irrelevance, they assert that nowadays the playwright as truth-teller is, in their view, a dead duck. No dramatist, save Alan Ayckbourn, finds him- or herself anywhere near the centre of a decent-sized theatre's policy. Fifty years on, they are able triumphantly to boast that we have re-established a narcotic theatre of amiable revival, one which, hardly by coincidence, is run by career directors and bureaucrats, and in which the writers and actors hang on as the junior partners, hired and fired by their betters. These observers point with pride to the fact that the National Theatre has only sometimes been valued for its depiction of contemporary life. They prefer it in its most recent incarnation as a palace of operetta, and see no reason why a national theatre should not secede to a national Opera Comique. They are happy to celebrate the Royal Shakespeare Company's abandonment of any vestiges of their original motive for having a colony in London, namely the wish to do large-scale modern as well as classical work.

Above all, enemies of John are delighted that the most important new indigenous art form of the twentieth century, the single television play – to which John contributed and which was used to such effect, and with such reach, by writers like David Mercer and Dennis Potter – was first vandalised and then purposely eliminated by post-modernist hooligans at the BBC. In their short-sighted eagerness to stamp out individual voices, channel controllers managed, to their own considerable harm, to rob public service television of the only thing which made it different from other television enterprises. By a paradox, in fact, they destroyed the most effective argument they had for the licence fee. When the wounded soldier Robert Lawrence discharges himself from military hospital in Charles Wood's 1989 Falklands film *Tumbledown* and sets off alone in his wheelchair in a bid for freedom, then not only are you witnessing the final evolution of the Osborne hero – the man with, this time literally, half the back of his head falling out, raging against history, refusing comfort – but you are also present at the moment when the BBC resolves that henceforward, when you want distinctive drama, they will buy it for you from HBO.

And yet. For all that, for all the long years of compromise, it remains my conviction that something of John's great dream refuses to go away. Throughout my childhood, on the few occasions that he returned to our home, my father warned me to take notice that as a merchant seaman he was part of a dying profession. His experience had proved to him that large ocean liners would soon cease to plough their way to Australia, taking bullet-jawed military to India and white dinner-jacketed racists to the Far East. The world of mah-jong, mulligatawny and pink gin could not, he said, be with us for long. Dad implored me on no account to consider throwing away my life, as he feared he had his, by entering a trade with such an uncertain future. I obeyed. Instead I entered the British theatre. Now I find myself, it seems, still manning the poop deck of my own Peninsular & Orient. I can hear a few desultory games of quoits being played on deck – I hear scattered applause and the odd shout of encouragement – and somewhere in the bowels of the ship it sounds as if a few suburban parties in knee-length taffeta and penguin suits are still glassy-eyed, dancing to the keening melodies of fifty-year-old musicals. At the bow, the gulls circle, waiting for scraps. You may see things either way. Yes, theatre culture has been significantly weakened since Osborne's appearance. And yet it is also an astonishment, a miracle, a ravishment that living theatre has survived at all.

Seneca reminds us that death takes us piecemeal, not at a gulp. John's romantic attempt to go on throwing himself against the bars of the cage was not pretty, and, in my own view, it was also doomed. But, to his considerable credit, John went on writing, insisting on meaning, way beyond a point where the world thanked him for it. He did not, like his great contemporary Peter Brook, go into exile, where he would risk draining individual plays of any specific meaning or context to a point where each one was in danger of becoming the same play – a sort of universal hippy babbling which, at its worst, seems to convey nothing but fright of commitment. And nor did he, like Joan Littlewood, throw the whole boiling out of the window in understandable despair. For myself, I now identify with John, shamelessly. No question, as you get older, fiction gets harder. At my age, you spend a great deal more time feeling humiliated by the degree to which you are not Chekhov than you do celebrating the degree to which you are not Somerset Maugham.

'Don't touch shit even with gloves on,' wrote the Hungarian playwright, Ferenc Molnár. 'The gloves get shittier, the shit doesn't get any glovier.' The only help to us as we proceed, shitty and gloved, gloved and shitty, through life, is the example of those we have admired. I first met John in 1971 when we both had plays in the same season at the Royal Court. I sat on the steps with him in Sloane Square in the company of David Storey and E. A. Whitehead to have our photograph taken by the *Sunday Times*. John seemed shiningly confident. He had travelled only down the King's Road, but he appeared to have come from another world to my own. I was twenty-three. John was more expensively barbered than any man I had hitherto met and even his jacket was a work of art. I was in awe, unable to speak. A few words then, from me, would, I now realise, have been worth far more to him than the six thousand I am offering today. The silence between us was profound. We shook hands hopelessly and parted. I thought it was his job to say something. Only now do I understand it was mine.

DAVID HARE